HELLRAISER
THE TOLL
AND OTHER STORIES

MARK ALAN MILLER

www.encyclopocalypse.com

CONTENTS

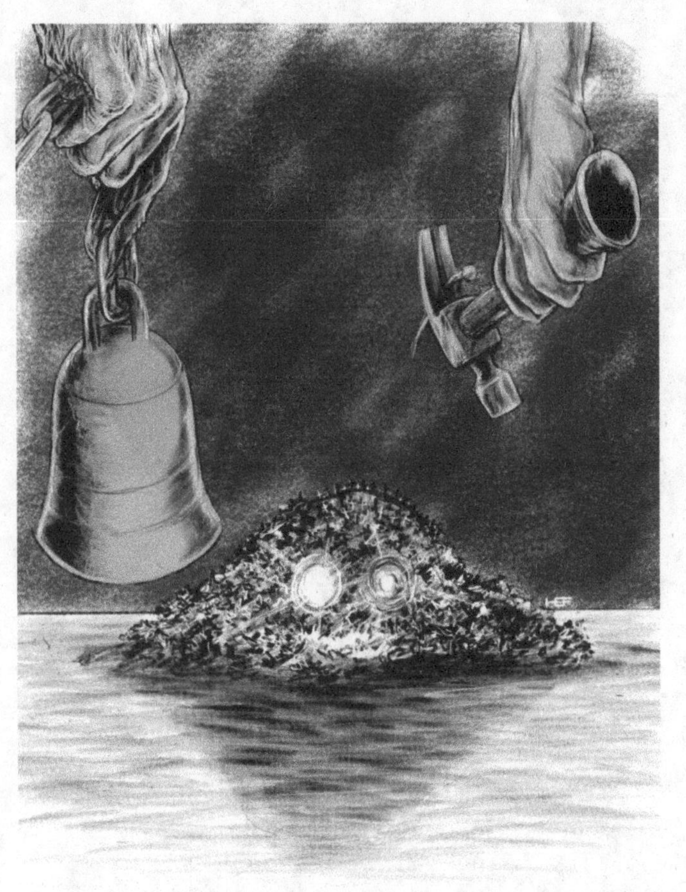

The founders of a new colony, whatever utopia of human virtue and happiness they might originally project, have invariably recognized it among their earliest practical necessities to allot a portion of the virgin soil as a cemetery, and another portion as the site of a prison.

— NATHANIEL HAWTHORNE

THE TOLL - PROLOGUE

-1-

For all the prisoners who'd passed through the walls of the colony, the Big House had been a grand and permanent place. It was, however, all an illusion. The ground floor was framed using old timbers brought from the mainland for that specific purpose. It was ugly but strong, with wood panels used to create an illusion of sturdiness.

The island upon which the faux fortress stood had been named twice. First by the missionaries who had discovered them as they fled the leprosy and the insanity of the mainland. There, finding refuge from the consuming disease that had almost destroyed them, they had named it Salvation Island in honor of the escape from death the rock had afforded them.

But the Salvation the island offered had only been temporary. Just a few years later, the land was once again deserted and prepared for its second baptism. In the middle of the nineteenth century the French government, looking for a place to ship the country's most vicious and unrepentant prisoners, had elected the name Guiana, effectively turning the land into a legitimate part of the French Empire.

Having failed with the honest, Mother France was obliged to turn to the dishonest. In 1852, the government under Napoleon III built a penal colony, with its administrative offices on the mainland, that left the island as the ultimate place of exile, punishment, and if all else failed, execution.

The island was a little piece of Hell, or so those who ended up there testified. Every day, great flocks of black birds rose up from the trees as the sun turned bloody and started to sink away. It seemed that the birds were forever buying into some grand delusion; that the sun was dying away forever, and once it was gone, the island would permanently belong to the night and so then to the maker of night: the Devil. Fitting, for it was he who had given his name to that rock, of course. What the missionaries had originally called Salvation Island, was now deemed The Devil's Island.

-2-

The Penal Colony which was built into the damned rock did not last. Though the French government did what it could to disguise the atrocities there, word got out. The horrors of incarceration on Devil's Island became news; and soon the governments around the world were demanding that the French act like a civilized nation, and purge this filth from their judicial system in the name of honor. The last prisoners left the island in 1952. That is to say, the last living prisoners. Thousands remained behind, buried in shallow graves of the pungent earth of the Island's cemeteries. The dead had each been marked by simple wooden crosses when they'd been buried, all except the suicides. The crosses had mostly gone now - rotted away into the same earth where those whose names had once been painted upon them were also rotting.

But the island was not deserted. Shortly after its closing, tourists with a taste for the macabre began visiting the island. Realizing there was some money to be made from their handmade Hell, the French government helped the rehabilitation of the island. The places of shame — the tiny cells where prisoners had been kept in solitary, seeing no human face nor hearing a human voice sometimes for a year or even more — were hosed clean and the heavy doors re-hung, so that a visitor might get to pretend what it felt like to be locked away in such tiny, airless confines, with not even a Bible for solace or distraction.

It was surprising how many men, having been in the cell no more than a minute or a minute and a half, were suddenly overtaken by panic. It was a sight that might have offered some bitter entertainment for the ghosts of those who had once endured the real solitude of those cells, decades before. But in truth, very few phantoms wandered the island. There was another spirit that had driven off the remains of other, simpler souls. He had been one of the prisoners there, for a time, though nobody was entirely certain what he'd done to earn his years of punishment amongst the damned. There were some who spoke of him having the same name as that of a famous toymaker, Phillipe Lemarchand, even though the toymaker in question had been born in 1784. But no definitive record of his demise had ever been located, which served only to fan the flames of conspiracy.

The question did not much vex the minds of those

who studied the period and the men who defined it. Lemarchand was simply a maker of whimsical toy mechanisms; scarcely worthy of the kind of discussion that a Napoleon might have deserved. When his name did occasionally come up in debates over the politics and entertainments of this period in French history, it was usually to speak of the bizarre rumors that had brought the man down.

Lemarchand had been a golden boy, almost literally—his mechanical birds and animals usually forged from gold at the expense of his noble patrons. But those rich men of influence who had bought Lemarchand's gilded singing birds and boxes for their mistresses could not defend him from the rumors of satanic dealings. These were, despite the rise of Reason, still times haunted by superstition, and no man – especially one as skilled and rich as Lemarchand – could escape the accusing fingers of his jealous competitors.

There was nothing in the reports that emerged from the agents of the ever-changing powers during those years that clearly told of Lemarchand's fate. In one court document he was recorded as condemned to life in prison for dealings with unholy powers. In another, there was an account of his being freed from imprisonment by the very mechanical birds that had raised him to such heights of celebrity. But none of this was certain except that an even deeper question lay beneath these uncertainties: what use could a maker of songbirds have had for the Devil? Or more strangely still, what use might the Devil have had for him?

What are you hiding? No one ever asks that.

— Sarah Vowell

THE TOLL -
PART ONE

-1-

There was only one letter in the morning mail. It was addressed to Christina Fidanza, which was the name she had been using since she'd had her problems with the Cenobites that had pursued her from the Wastes through Paris. Even though she'd become as expert as any criminal in the means by which a fugitive moved undetected around the world — she had two dozen passports, some exceptionally realistic, others only good for a quick glance, plus the encoded addresses of eleven safe houses around Europe and North America; all sanctuaries from pursuers — she did not believe for an instant that she was safe.

Her pursuers were likely to be able to come after her using the most sophisticated of means, which somewhat paradoxically meant the most ancient; reading her whereabouts not on images sent by satellites, but by far more arcane methods. Methods grotesque and cruel. Since she had first encountered the workings of Hell, in a house on Lodovico Street, not more than two miles from the flat she now occupied, she had become knowledgeable in the ways that worked behind the skin of the world (ways to find someone such as herself, for instance) that were so coldly cruel that even now, nearly thirty years later, she still woke most nights, drenched in sweat, the somber voice of the cold man with the nails in his face echoing in her ears. Somehow, twice, she had escaped his grasp, and the grasps of his acolytes. But no matter how far she fled, they were always with her. And she knew, if they ever wanted her back – really wanted her – they would have her.

In the end, there was only one who might one day choose to finish the business which had begun when Frank Cotton had come back to Lodovico Street.

She had barely looked at the letter that had been addressed to the woman she'd become since departing Paris. As happened so often, a drizzle of memories had quickly become monsoonal, and she was blinded to the present by pasts she'd either lived or dreamed she'd lived. Had she truly spoken to the demon with the cold touch all those years ago?

She forced herself back to the letter she held in her hand, leaving the demon's bitter breath somewhere behind her - and somehow also ahead. The letter was several pages long, handwritten with a pen that was swiftly running out of ink. From the letterhead, she saw that it was from somebody she'd never heard of, a Doctor of Theology in a Midwestern University by the name of Joseph Lansing. But her ignorance of him did not reach in the opposite direction.

All my life, he explained, *I have had an abhorrence of cliché. And yet here I am writing what will almost certainly be my first and last letter to you, and I find that no words suit better my present predicament than those of the weary cliché:*

'Burn after reading.'

Christina Fidanza, born Kirsty Cotton, glanced back up at the letterhead: at the plain authoritative design and address, all of which suggested that however strangely this letter had begun, there was a good chance the man who'd written it was indeed a Doctor of Theology. This fact, of course, guaranteed nothing by way of sanity. And often quite the opposite.

Kirsty reigned herself in from her wandering thoughts again.

"Read the damn letter," she said to herself.

If you are reading this, then I am dead, he'd written. *Or at least I haven't long to live.*

As her eyes traced the words on the paper she was struck with a feeling of déjà vu, and her mind began a journey back to her childhood, when a handwritten letter of a different nature had also made her feel profoundly uncomfortable.

––––––

At the age of six and a half, Kirsty remembered, along with the other half-dozen kids in the Sunday School Miss Pryor taught at St. Patrick's on Germaine Road, Kirsty had written a letter to God. Miss Pryor had said it was very important that they say what they felt. It wasn't right for anyone else to tell you what to say to God, because everything, even a letter, was a prayer, and they were between you and God. But, there was one thing she wanted them all to make sure they put in their letters. They should all be sure to ask for something for Mankind.

"And why should we ask for something for Mankind?" she had asked. "Kirsty. What about you?"

Kirsty had shaken her head. She remembered it very clearly, because she'd done it so violently. She'd wanted it to make a muddle of her thoughts so that she wouldn't remember too well what Miss Pryor had said, and then she wouldn't have to lie to her Sunday School teacher. But no, the thoughts had stayed all neat and tidy. And when she stopped shaking her head, Miss Pryor was still staring at her with those pale-lidded eyes of hers, and said:

"I think you do know, Kirsty."

"I don't know," she said. "Because, you told us what to tell God, Miss Pryor, even though you said nobody should do that. Does that mean you're going to Hell?"

Kirsty kept staring at those pale-lidded eyes, knowing that she had caught Miss Pryor in her own trap. She saw the teacher try to pull her eyes away from Kirsty's gaze, but Kirsty refused to give them up. She was aware, even though she was staring straight into Miss Pryor's eyes that her teacher's face was getting blotchy-red. Her cheeks, parts of her neck, even her forehead.

"Alright, Kirsty," she said. "I think we've all had enough of that. You can stop it now."

"Stop what, Miss?"

"You know."

"No I don't."

"Yes you do!" Miss Pryor said, and she hit Kirsty so hard across her face that she knocked her out of her chair.

———

Kirsty cut the memory off there and finding herself halfway through the letter with no idea what she'd read, started reading the letter from the beginning.

I know it must seem strange, getting a letter out of the blue from someone you've never heard of, but don't worry;

all of your secrets are safe with me. I had a lot of your secrets in my files here at the University, but they've all been shredded now. I realized I had to do that. And I just wanted you to know, if any name ever comes up in the future, and one of these sons of bitches starts to tell you the things they heard from me, it's all bullshit, because they heard nothing.

I know how those bastards work. They tell you that they know stuff when they don't know shit. Excuse my language, but I learned early on in my dealings with Hell that a familiarity with the scatological is essential. Excrement is the language of the Wastes, is it not? The damned place is called the Wastes, after all.

My apologies. I truly don't seem to have been able to hold on to a single coherent thought for more than a moment without it slipping away from me. It's the strangest thing.

Let me return to my reason for writing to you in the first place. I am cognizant of the situation I potentially put you in by making contact with you given that certain parties are tracking my mail. But I assure you that if they are, then all of your correspondences are also being tracked. They know where you are. The only question is where do we stand on their list of priorities?

Apparently neither of us stands higher because we are still alive to tell the tale. Or in my case, to ask the question, which is this: What do you know about the last years of the life of Phillipe Lemarchand? I'm sure we're both familiar with the same basic details. The man was a brilliant craftsman, worked in gold a lot, created songbirds for several of the monarchs of Europe, uncannily life-like, and that at some point in his career he was commissioned to fashion puzzle boxes, which became known as the Lament Configurations.

The puzzle boxes made music just as the birds did. But they did something else too. They opened the door to that desolate part of Hell called the Wastes, where the labyrinth of the Cenobites stood. And that thing worked a monstrous magic, by all accounts. I know you witnessed one of those doors opening. I never did. I only read descriptions of how Lemarchand was able to turn his hand to working with beauty and melody…

The letter lost coherence, such as it could be called, after that, as Lansing once again fell before the whim of his arbitrary thoughts.

There was only one other thing of any importance in the letter, and it was casually dropped within the last of its seven manic pages. *There are other ways for the demons to cross a threshold,* Lansing had remarked, *besides someone solving some antiquated puzzle box.* And the way he heard it, one of those ways was going to become apparent very soon. If his information was correct, then the thresholds would be uncovered by whatever means were going to become available. And it wasn't going to be long before a lot of curious, but presumably wicked souls, were going to be utilizing them. The message was clear: the world was going to change very quickly, unless Kirsty was willing to help.

-2-

Kirsty wandered the house for the next several hours, her thoughts even more chaotic than they'd been of late. Eventually she decided to bite the bullet. She wouldn't normally entertain such manic missives, but Lansing knew things about her that she couldn't ignore. She would call Lansing and find out whether he even existed. And if it proved to be another one of Hell's house calls, she knew how to make herself disappear. It was the only life she had known for decades.

She dialed the number on the letterhead.

The recorded voice, that of a woman in her fifties, Kirsty thought, provided little information.

"Hello, you have reached the offices of Doctor Joseph Lansing. If you wish to leave a message, please press—"

Kirsty hung up the phone. It was only when she'd put the phone down that she realized she was clammy with sweat, and her heart was hammering. She felt a little ridiculous now. So what if a total stranger had sent her a vaguely apocalyptic letter? It didn't contain any actual information of great urgency, nor did she perceive any kind of threat. Certainly nothing to explain why she had become so agitated. Was it that someone had found her, and seemingly knew of her past? Was it simply the fact that she dialed the number that had stirred her up, as though by calling this stranger about some rumor of an ambiguous possibility, she was somehow lending this whole fiction a veracity it did not deserve, or worse yet, leaving herself vulnerable in some way she had not yet fathomed?

She tried to distract herself from Phillipe Lemarchand and the puzzle box by doing some mundane work around her apartment. There were bills to be paid, and various unanswered correspondences to be dealt with. But her heart wasn't in it. She couldn't keep her mind focused on the purpose in front of her. Her thoughts were returning to that house on Lodovico Street where a hunt had become the unwelcome subject of her entire life thereafter.

It was love that had troubled her, love that had shown her the road to Hell. It had been her profoundest hope that the road was one she would never have to walk again; but Lansing's letter had cast doubt on that hope. So now her mind went back and back to Lodovico Street, and to the last man she had loved without conditions – her father; the man whose life had been lost there, under circumstances she still had difficulty making sense of. The man was Larry Cotton, married to a beautiful, terrible woman by the name of Julia. Julia had never loved her husband. Kirsty saw the contempt his own wife felt for Larry every time Julia glanced at him. But Larry never saw it. He worshiped Julia. She could do no wrong. When she'd sickened and refused to tell Larry what was wrong with her, he'd turned in desperation to Kirsty. Could she not speak with Julia one day, and maybe get the truth out of her?

Kirsty had done as her father had asked. But she'd found no truth. Though her father had told Kirsty his wife was pale and sickly, she was anything but. Kirsty found Julia looking flushed, sweaty, and agitated. She looked, Kirsty thought, like a woman who was entertaining male company: a suspicion that had been further supported by a stranger's coat hanging within sight of the doorstep where Kirsty stood. Julia had been in no mood for niceties.

Kirsty remembered with particular clarity what had happened as she'd retreated from Julia and the place she called home; how very strongly she'd had the sense of being scrutinized, and how she'd looked back and known somehow that it wasn't Julia who was watching her from one of the upper windows, but her secret lover, whoever he was.

Only later would she discover the vile truth: that the lover Julia was entertaining in the house that afternoon had been her own uncle, Larry's brother, Frank Cotton, a man whose exploits — as an explorer of all things extreme and forbidden — were believed to have ended his life. In a sense, this was true. In pursuit of experiences beyond anything his flesh had ever known, Larry's brother had purchased from a felon in Berlin - a man called Kircher who had been responsible for the blinding of a two-month-old baby and the murder of the infant's mother – a box, legendary in unholy circles, known as the Lament Configuration.

Then he set about opening it, and he quickly learned the error of his choices. The place of erotic atrocities he'd hoped to discover instead opened a doorway into the Wastes of Hell, and he, thanks to the box, had become the prisoner of its overlords, the Order of the Gash, a sadistic sect of demons known as Cenobites.

Kirsty only discovered all of this later, when she'd accidentally summoned the creatures up with her own fingers. There were four of these creatures, their bodies slashed and sutured beyond recognition, the wounds decorated and displayed as though they were things of beauty.

Kirsty would have become their prey as Frank had, if she hadn't solved the mystery of Frank Cotton's life after death. Frank had escaped his captors with the aid of Julia, who had nourished him with the life-blood of the few hopeful lovers she'd seduced to Lodovico Street through the promise of a little lunchtime adultery. In the end, Frank and Julia took Larry's life, and then his skin, in an attempt to hide Frank in perpetuity from his tormentors. But like a clever innocent in a nursery tale, Kirsty had tricked Frank into offering up the most crucial scrap of information in the invisible presence of those tormentors: his own name. It didn't matter whose face he'd stolen to conceal himself. He was Frank Cotton.

"Hush now," he'd said ot her, brandishing his switchblade. "Everything's alright. Frank's here. Your dear old uncle Frank."

He would have taken her life a moment later, but his attention had been distracted by the sound of a tolling bell. She had known its origin the instant it began to sound. She could smell the bitter air of the Infernal place from which it had emanated. They came swiftly. And when they did, they took him. The whole affair was after a gruesome, violent conflict that had left her with nightmares of the house on Lodovico Street for as long as she could remember.

There was no logic to what she decided to do next. But then she knew from harsh experience that the world she had escaped from contained not a grain of logic. So it made sense, in such a world, to go back to Lodovico Street, and sniff the old place out.

-3-

A week later, Kirsty found herself standing in a neighborhood she hardly recognized. At first she thought she'd miscounted the houses, or that what had once been the Cotton residence had been so extensively renovated that she'd failed to spot it. But she walked back and forth along the street again and again, studying the houses and paving stones beneath her feet, looking for some tiny sign she found familiar. But there was nothing. The house had literally vanished without a trace; its very existence, or any evidence thereof, erased in every way. There could only be one explanation: some force, angelic or infernal, had scratched out the place where the threshold to Hell had stood. The moment she accepted this — not as a possibility, but as gospel — her eyes recalculated Lodovico Street, and she saw the evidence of where the house had been torn away. The street had been crudely refitted so that the paving stones almost matched. The crack in the earth where the house had been uprooted and carried away would have been undetectable had she not implemented the more metaphysical calculations.

She didn't linger to study the signs, however. Who knew what kinds of eyes still watched over the spot, and might have called down forces to interrogate her on the matter of her curiosity? Careful to conceal her awareness, she went on her way. But as she walked on, she found that her awakening to the illusions on Lodovico Street had changed the world beyond it; or rather, because her eyes had changed, she now saw her surroundings as they truly were. She chose, for reasons of safety, to walk to her hotel by way of the busiest streets. It was a little after four, and the first escapees from the St. Francis Elementary School padded the number of pedestrians along her route, their raucous laughter and shrill shrieks a welcome reminder of a safer world.

Her changed eyes saw the same wing she'd seen where the Cotton house had stood. Everywhere she looked, she now saw cracked flagstones poorly fitted back together, the bricks in walls mismatched where the schoolchildren wove about one another as they ran, squealing with ignorant delight.

She was three blocks from the corner of the street where she turned off to make her way back to her room when the first drops of rain began to fall. The kids stopped racing each other and instead sped off down the street to outrun the storm. Kirsty picked up her pace, and lowered her head. The rain — chilled by the gusts of wind driving it — was blown against her face. She squinted against the needle jabs of ice water and when she next looked up there had been another substantial emptying of the pavements, as adults cut short whatever business they might have had in these last cold hours of the afternoon, and were hurrying away to the shelter of the Underground or the occasional cab that had not yet been claimed.

Kirsty reached the corner of the street and glanced back. To Kirsty's recollection, it had been one of the few streets in the neighborhood that had genuine charm. Many years before days at the Cotton house, some far-sighted city official had planted trees along both sides of this street, and they had prospered in the decades since. But while Kirsty was busy trying to outrun her past, someone had taken a chainsaw and had cut the branches back with such brutality that the work resembled amputation rather than pruning.

Kirsty was feeling too vulnerable on this late afternoon to bear the sight of these butchered trees, so she turned her back on the street. But as she did so she heard the sound of somebody running nearby on the rain-soaked sidewalk. She tried to get a fix on the runner, and caught sight of a slim, dark, bald figure on the left-hand side of the street, racing in and out of the trees carrying a darkness towards her as he came. He was chanting, she heard, the meaning of his call at first inexplicable, rendered only more complex by its own echo, which doubled back on itself. But when she held her breath a moment and listened more carefully the simple obscenity which found her ears was all too easily understood:

"Fuck! Fuck! Fuck! Fuck! Fuck! Fuck! Fuck! Fuck! Fuck!"

She could not yet see his face as he briefly emerged from the desiccated trees, but she quickly became accustomed to the rhythm with which he was appearing and disappearing, and was able to predict the moment of his next appearance. The only certain thing about him was the clarity with which he repeated the word:

"FUCK! FUCK! FUCK! FUCK!"

With each utterance a very fine thread of lightning leapt up out of his mouth, spreading out, and igniting his bony torso as it escaped his lips.

"FUCK! FUCK! FUCK!" he yelled.

The speed with which he was weaving his way towards her, and the volume of his shout, made it very difficult for her to resist fleeing before his approach, but at the end of the street directly beneath the last of the sycamores, she halted and stood her ground. The Runner was instantly intimidated by this and he stopped in his tracks. The lightning that had been so incandescent when he'd been running at her lost its brilliance. There was one last illumination that showed his face. Kirsty seemed then to see the sadness there that had not been visible before. Then, the last of the light died away and he simply stood there, the rain slapping on the pavement around him.

She watched him for a moment, and then turned and walked away. She had no fear of him now. No doubt he was some form of demonic entity, and no doubt his origins lay somewhere with that far greater evil that had appeared in Lodovico Street. The fact that he was fiend, she knew, more or less guaranteed her safety once she turned the corner. Demons were territorial. More than likely the Runner had been given the sycamores to watch over as they rotted in their living roots. This was what she told herself as she pressed on. She did not look back, but turned the corner of the street and left the Runner and his sycamores to their mutual decay.

．　．　．

-4-

By the time Kirsty reached her room, the light shower had become a deluge, numbing her face and hands. Her fingers were so chilled that she twice dropped her key before successfully getting it into the lock and turned. Once inside, she got herself dry and warm as quickly as possible. She turned on the heating, and grabbed a towel from the bathroom to dry off her hair, sloughing off her sodden shoes as she did so and padding on bare feet across the cold tiles. As she went to pick up the towel, some spasm in her cortex brought the vision of the Runner back into her mind's eye. She saw him there looking melancholy as the rain pelted him, the last frail fragment of lightning illuminating his face. She realized then that she needed a drink. She went to the mini-fridge and took out a small bottle of brandy. Her Grandmother (God bless her pragmatic, Puritan soul) had remarked on several occasions that brandy was useful in every emergency, especially death.

She could find no glasses, but she didn't care. She unscrewed the little cap and offered up a little toast before she put the bottle to her lips:

"Grandma, if you're up there, keep an eye on me, will you? I've got problems."

No question, she was in trouble. Whatever she hoped to learn at Lodovico Street, whatever she may have gained by way of visions, none of it was worth the price of attentions she was beginning to fear she'd just drawn in her direction.

Things were in motion, like water being drained at a great rate out of a tub — only a huge tub, a tub maybe the size of the world — and she felt like a scrap of a bit of a remnant of nothing — being carried down, round and round, down and down, into the place where the rest of the world was going. And wherever that place was, she knew it wasn't good.

The ever-irritated wind gusted against the window again. She thought of the Runner. Was he still out there, she wondered, trying to find some small measure of shelter beneath those trees, which his bosses had surely had their hands in destroying, leaving him naked and cold?

The image that had appeared in her head in turn flowed on into another image, one which she had first encountered in a history lesson in high school. It was the obligatory grainy scratched footage from a concentration camp, taken not by its liberators but by some minor monster who had considered the spectacle of dying Jews worthy of home movies. The casual way in which this scene had been filmed had made a powerful impression upon Kirsty at the age of fourteen. She had been haunted by the image for weeks after the lesson and had found herself asking the inevitable question: what would I have done? Would she have simply set her jaw and defied the icy rain to erode her hope, knowing that she would be shown no mercy by heaven or earth, or would she have perished - dropped into the dirty snow, giving up all hope of a brighter time while the black smoke billowed from the cremation chimney above the camp?

Somehow people got through these terrors. Somehow they convinced themselves that all they needed was the tiniest of hopes, the smallest of cracks through which to escape into a better world that was waiting for them tomorrow. Was she amongst them? Was there a better tomorrow to be had? She didn't know.

It was time to find some answers. There weren't,

unfortunately, a lot of places to look or people to ask. One of the few might be Lansing. She grabbed herself another bottle of brandy from the mini-fridge and finished changing out of her damp clothes into some dry ones. Then she again called the number in Minnesota. This time somebody picked up the phone. It was a man's voice.

"Joe Lansing's office," said the voice. "How may I help you?"

"I'd like to speak to Dr. Lansing if he's available," Kirsty said.

"Depends who wants to talk to him," the man replied.

"My name's Kirsty, I received a letter a little while ago."

"Okay. What do you need?"

"I think you know what I need."

"I'm afraid I don't have time for this. Right now I have some people in my office and they need to talk to me."

There was something about the tone of the man's voice that made Kirsty uneasy. Not for herself, but for the man who was four thousand miles away. It was her unease that kept her from pressing the questions any further. All she said was:

"Things are rather urgent where I am. In fact they're a little dangerous. I've got about an hour's worth of packing to do and then I'm leaving. If you wouldn't mind telling Dr. Lansing that, I would be very grateful."

"Why don't you just call me back when you're done?" he said. And without waiting for her to reply, he hung up.

-5-

. . .

Kirsty had moved too many times to be challenged by the organizational routine. It was a job that needed to be done, and it needed to be done fast — in this case, as was so often true, very fast — so that she could be ready to depart as soon as she made her follow up call to Lansing. She fortified her maneuvers with a third brandy and then got about the all-too-familiar task of fitting the important things in her life into one medium-sized suitcase and one smaller bag with a number of compartments for papers and clothes.

She had a much-used large leather wallet which had served for many years as a receptacle for everything that she absolutely needed to get herself out of one country and into another, out of danger and into whatever approximation of safety the world would ever offer her; that was the first item into one of the compartments of the smaller bag. It was followed by a selection of less necessary, but still useful items, including several pieces of forged paperwork, allowing her in and out of countries as a national.

Had anybody assessed the contents of these various pouches they would probably have assumed Kirsty was in the espionage business. In a sense, she was. The enemy was spiritual, not national, but the dangers were as real and as sudden as anything she might have encountered had her enemies been things of guns and steel, rather than hell and damnation.

Kirsty had first heard hell's bell tolling in the attic room at the top of the house on Lodovico Street. It had signaled the approach of the greatest source of evil she hoped she would ever meet - the demon with the bitter breath; the creature she could only think of as The Cold Man – perhaps the most notorious member of the Order of the Gash. Though she had never seen the bell, nor the steeple in which that bell hung, nor what unholy force caused it to ring, she had seen the mechanism which sent a message to that steeple from this world. It was a box, a golden box, reputedly fashioned by a French maker of automatons by the name of Phillipe Lemarchand.

She thought of Frank, whose desire to know more, taste more, own more of the world's supply of experience than was his right to possess, had brought one of the boxes Lemarchand had fashioned into the house on Lodovico Street. Kirsty had held it in her hand. It had been heavy, she remembered. Her hand still knew its weight as though the flesh of her palm would always be haunted by the holding of it.

And the creature it eventually summoned went by many names. To those foolish or suicidal enough to indulge in insult, he was called Pinhead. Kirsty had thought it was an idiot name the first time she'd heard it, and had not changed her opinion since. She didn't doubt that those who had first used the name had done so believing it would somehow take away from his power. But no. The Pinhead was a poisonous flower by any name.

Besides, like most of the entities that haunted the Wastes, the Cenobite owned more than one name. Many demons had half a dozen or more. Pinhead had been given his name from the ranks of nails that were driven in a symmetrical pattern over his entire head, from the line of his jaw up over his dour and weary face to the spot at the base of his naked skull where a hook kept the flesh taut. She was certain he went by other names. She'd never know them, but it mattered little. To her, he was The Cold Man.

She realized she should have been talking to Lansing by now.

The Cold Man…

She looked at the clock beside the bed. She had to call.

The Cold Man…

This was all about him. It had always been about him. She was his unfinished business, she knew. An irritant left over from his manipulations of Frank Cotton. More than likely if he had any intentions regarding her, they were to kill her. Isn't that what you did with unfinished business? You got rid of it. Shredded it. Threw it in the fire. Smothered it.

She buried her thought of the Cold Man and dialed the number. As the call went through, the connections clicking and whirring across the miles between them, she reached for the television remote and dialed down the volume on the news channel she'd been watching.

The clicking stopped. A connection was made. Kirsty dialed the last of the volume to silence and waited for contact to be made.

It was a recording that replied, not life.

-6-

"Hello, you've reached the offices of Dr. Joseph Lansing. If you wish to leave a message…"

Why not, this time? If she was going to die at the hands of the Cold Man anyway, what did it matter if she left Lansing a message or not? Certainly an innocent message, telling Lansing that she'd called, could cause no furor.

"Dr. Lansing? I know I'm late calling you back—" (Shit! Why had she said that? Well, it was done now.) "—and—and I just—and—" (What should she say now? Her wits always seemed to fail her when the abyss of the answering machine stared back at her.)

"—I guess there's nothing more I can really—"

"Kirsty! Where have you been?"

"I'm sorry! I-"

"I have to make this very quick."

"I'm listening."

"It's the Pinhead."

That name. It was exactly what she didn't want to hear. It was a stone in her stomach.

"What about him?"

"I know where he is."

"Okay." Kirsty kept her silence a moment. Then: "What's that got to do with me?"

"I need you to help me deal with him."

"Why me?" Kirsty said. "And come to that, why you?"

"Because if not, the world will end."

Lansing's voice was a monotone. Not for a moment did Kirsty doubt he knew what he was talking about. But the urgency, which had been in his voice at the beginning of the conversation, had given way to something else. She wasn't quite sure what it was, but she listened for it when next he spoke.

"They're listening to us," he said. "Probably they've been on to us all along. After all, I hear you had an encounter with something this afternoon."

He knew about the Runner. How?

"Where did you hear about him?"

"It's in the air, Kirsty. The final act is about to be performed by the one who stays to watch the curtain fall. Somebody who can afford to buy the theatre and tear it down. Leave it empty ground."

It was a strange little metaphor. But Kirsty was not even mildly tempted to ask him what the fuck he meant by it.

"I can't give you explanations," he said. "It would be too dangerous. You either have to trust me, or not."

"And if not?"

"*You* tell me."

"Alright. Just one question then, if I help you to deal with him, does that mean I get my life back?"

"Life or death," he said. "You'll get one or the other."

Curiously, this wasn't such a bad option. She'd reached the end of her rope. Better to play in the Final Act, even though she didn't yet know the words, than to meander on in the hope that sooner or later somebody would kill the lights.

"That sounds about right. What do you need?"

"Have you ever heard of Devil's Island?"

"After Lodovico Street," Kirsty said, "I researched everything with the word devil in it. Of course I know. The Devil's Island. One of the worst prisons in the history of human cruelty. A French penal colony off the coast of French Guiana. What about it?"

"That's where he is."

"And?"

"Do you have enough money to purchase a ticket there?"

"You want me to fly to an island the size of my bed because the Cold Man is waiting for me there?"

"Interesting association of words," Lansing said. "Your bed and the Cold Man."

"Don't even," she warned.

"Just an observation."

"Say I go? What then?"

"Keep his attention long enough to bring this sad story to a happy end."

"You're kidding."

"About?"

"That there's a happy ending?"

"We have to believe it's still possible. It's very remote perhaps, but still…"

"Yes," she said. "I know. That's all I'm going to get with so little time."

"You and I both know that to him you are the Grand Note in the Final Chorus. If anybody can hold him there to listen for a few more seconds while the stars align, it's you."

When your time comes to die, be not like those whose hearts are filled with fear of death, so that when their time comes they weep and pray for a little more time to live their lives over again in a different way. Sing your death song, and die like a hero going home.

— Tecumseh

THE TOLL -
PART TWO

-1-

It took Kirsty the better part of forty hours to get from her room in London to the Devil's Island.

She got a cab to take her out to Heathrow, where she caught an Air France flight to Paris. The London flight brought her into Charles de Gaulle Airport, while her flight to French Guiana left from Orly. That meant another cab ride, this time from one airport to the other. At Orly she checked in for the longest leg of her journey, which was the nine-hour trip between continents. Kirsty had a plastic glass of red wine with the meal that was served about a third of the way into the flight. It was better wine than she'd expected, and the when the stewardess came round to offer her a refill she happily accepted.

"Am I going to regret this?" she said.

"It's supposed to be good for you. Isn't that what they're saying these days? And if you want to sleep for a while just let me know and I'll bring you an extra couple of pillows. We've got plenty; the flight's barely half-full."

The wine worked well as a soporific. She felt the tensions in her body ease away, her eyelids so heavy she could not have kept them open if she'd wanted to. She lost her hold on the world of solid things, and at last gave in to a dreamless sleep.

-2-

The ship approached the island from the open ocean, and there weighed anchor. When it did so, the ship's solitary passenger disembarked, transferring to a smaller vessel: a black boat which had room only for two oarsmen, and its passenger. She arrived on the island wondering what new form Hell would reveal to her, and how it was possible that she never grew accustomed to the feeling of terror, even though she always carried it with her.

-3-

"It's very good you came today," Madame Rembert, who owned the two-bedroom hotel, which offered the island's only accommodation, explained to Kirsty. "Yesterday, I was on the mainland, at a funeral. I run the premises on my own, which is not easy for a woman of eighty-one..." She left this information as bait dangling in the hot, whispering air. Kirsty allowed herself a little smile in disbelief that she had come all this way, only to meet a woman who had the same tricks for winning a compliment as her own mother. She concealed the smile, and went for the bait.

"Eighty-one? I find that hard to believe. You don't look a day over seventy."

Madame Rembert was briefly radiant. "I have so much to offer a man, even now. But the men here? Ha! They're either dead or insane."

"May I ask—"

"Why I'm here?" she said. Then she called to someone. "Walter."

A small grayish man, with deep grooves running the length of his face, presented himself. He was instructed to take Kirsty's bag to her room, and to pour two glasses of sherry to be served on the veranda.

"Walk with me," she said to Kirsty.

As she spoke, she walked out of the door of the little room that served as the hotel's office, and waved her hand at the scenery, or what passed for it. It was little more than a green wall, in truth. The jungle would have overtaken Madame Rembert's little hotel long ago had it not been for the men who had been working up and down the perimeter for the hour and half Kirsty had been here. As they went about their business, Kirsty exited the office, following after Madame Rembert, and headed left down the narrow walkway, in the direction she'd seen the old woman walk. The ancient, warped boards beneath her feet creaked as she progressed.

As the men went about their business, Kirsty stole a glance at the small collection of bizarre, almost child-like paintings of the jungle that lined the wall. They were curious things: landscapes depicting abstracted versions of the jungle and its birds. They seemed to pull the eye toward them, as though images or messages hidden deep beneath the paint yearned to break free. Kirsty shook them from her mind and turned a corner. There she saw Madame

Rembert sitting on the veranda, sipping sherry, watching the silent men shuffle up and down the edge of the property, keeping the jungle ever at a distance.

"Twenty yards," Madame Rembert said.

"What is?"

"The distance between the hotel and that." She raised a trembling hand in the direction of the jungle: the canopy of the trees, heavy with foliage, bowing to meet the knotted shrubs, which were overrun with plants and vines. Green, green, and more green. And where it wasn't green, black and flat.

"That wall." She sipped at her sherry as though this were a Sunday afternoon in some bourgeois suburb of Paris, not the sweltering wilds of the densest jungle in the world.

"It doesn't look very welcoming," Kirsty said.

"It isn't. I presume you came here out of some kind of curiosity about a place that has seen too much sorrow and too much death. It won't take you but a day to get your fill of it. That's all there is to see."

"There are other houses, though. I saw them down by the harbor."

"There are a few, yes. But fewer and fewer are occupied every year. The people who lived there have all died, and nobody claims the homes. Why would they?"

"Isn't that bad for business?"

"You think I give a damn about business? My husband Claude's buried here. That's the only reason I remain."

"What about the hotel?"

"Damn the hotel. I stay to be with Claude, until it's over and somebody puts me down the same hole. I wouldn't ever want him to be alone, you understand?"

"I suppose..."

Madame Rembert looked at Kirsty with the eyes of a born interrogator. "Could you leave the remains of somebody you loved here? Knowing what this island is?"

Kirsty paused, holding Madame Rembert's gaze as long as she could before looking back at the green wall. "I don't know what the island is yet," she said. Her reply didn't impress Madame Rembert much.

"Please, girl. You are not here to look at some old prison. You are here because you know more about the Devil than most. Isn't that right?"

"Maybe."

"If you want to play silly games, I will leave you to it," Madame Rembert said, starting to push herself up out of the creaking wicker chair in which she sat.

"You're right. And I don't want to play games any more than you do. I'm sorry. I'm uneasy, that's all."

"You have reason to be."

"Oh?" Kirsty returned her scrutiny to the old lady. Kirsty watched Madame Rembert enjoy her sham of indecision before she finally lowered herself back onto her weary creaking throne.

"You know what's best. I don't need to tell you," she said softly.

"Are you saying I shouldn't be here?"

"You see? You know without need of being told. If you wish, I will have Walter bring down your bag and I'll have him take you back down to the harbor and find you a boat to take you back to the mainland."

"Now?"

"Yes, now; of course, now. This is not a game."

"I know. I've seen."

"I know what you've seen. Your reputation precedes you," Madame Rembert said. "What happened on Lodovico Street became something repeated in bad times."

"How do you know about Lodovico Street?"

"It is my business to know these touchstones. Events like that when a law is defied — when Hell's law is defied — the defier becomes a powerful figure. I think of my Claude, who lived in the shadow of Hell for most of his life... how the knowledge of people like you existing in the world would've given him comfort. Even if you were not worthy of the gift you had been given. Even if you were just another..."

The words trailed away.

"Another?"

"...Sinner," Madame Rembert said very quietly.

"People seriously overuse that word," Kirsty said. She then turned her back on the woman and stepped back into the house. In the short time she'd been sitting outside with Madame Rembert the tropical night had fallen all too suddenly. Outside there'd been enough light left in the sky to keep things bright. In Madame Rembert's office, where the lamps were unlit, it was very dark now, and getting darker by the second. Kirsty stood on the threshold.

"Is there somebody else here?" she asked the darkness.

"It's just me," said a voice out of the shadows. "Walter."

He stepped into the only patch of light left in the room. His face was severe.

"What is it, Walter?" Rembert asked from outside without so much as looking his way.

"Something is here," Walter almost whispered and went to the small desk where the sign-in ledger was laid. He brought a key out of his pocket, and with an arthritic creak, went down onto his haunches and fumbled to get the key into a lock. Only then did he speak.

"Will you turn the lamp on, please?"

Now it was Kirsty who did the fumbling. By the time she found the lamp and the switch in the gloom, Walter had already opened the desk drawer and was bringing a metallic box, which rattled loudly when he set it on the desk. As he did so, he called to his employer, his voice now artificially loud to cover the noise of whatever he was doing. There was no answer from Madame. Walter glanced up at Kirsty, who glanced down at his handiwork. He had brought an antiquated gun out of the metal box and with nervous, ill-practiced fingers was attempting to put bullets into its chambers.

"Will you find out what Madame's doing, s'il vous plait?"

Kirsty went to the window and peered out, looking for Madame. The old lady's wicker chair was empty, however. The embroidered cushion on which she'd been sitting had been pulled off the chair in Rembert's haste to be up, and was lying on the steps that led down onto the poorly kempt lawn. As for Madame, Kirsty saw that she was walking slowly but intently towards the wall of trees, which was now completely shrouded in darkness.

"Well?" Walter said.

"She's going towards the trees. I think she's seen somebody."

"Shit, it's all happening," Walter said very quietly. He was still struggling to get the bullets into the gun, his frustration evident.

Kirsty's gaze went without her instruction to the wall behind the desk, where hung the largest of Claude Rembert's colorful portraits of the jungle. The true subject of this picture was not, however, the jungle or the golden birds, which had been featured so prominently in his other paintings. In the center of the poorly stretched canvas was a house, quite unlike anything that Kirsty had seen in her researches. It looked almost American Colonial in its style, the facade featuring six gold and black pillars, which supported an elaborate entryway. Located in the center, between the pillars, was a great door, its yawning mouth half open, but offering no glimpse of the interior of the estate. The mouth of a chimney rising high into the sky belched red cinders, the smoke rising higher and finally disappearing into the night sky.

There were never perfect moments to ask important questions, Kirsty knew. She also knew with sickening certainty that the house in Claude's masterwork was somehow an important part of her life. She couldn't shake the feeling that the paintings were screaming messages at her that she failed to grasp.

"The house," Kirsty said. "With the pillars."

"Burned down years ago," Walter replied coldly. "It had a huge furnace. It exploded." He glanced up at her, daring her to press any further. She knew it would get her nowhere. Instead she said:

"Can I help load the gun?"

"I'm almost done," Walter said. "See if you can find anything to use as a weapon in the cupboard over there."

"Alright," Kirsty said and she moved toward the cabinet, turning her back on Walter for the last time in her life.

-4-

• • •

Genevieve Rembert had been a very beautiful woman. And sometimes, sitting at her little dressing table some mornings, if the light was kind, she saw a very distant memory of that beauty she once held. And she was very sad for the life that would never be hers to live again, nor the happiness to be had.

She thought of her changing reflection as she walked towards the wall of jungle that marked the boundary of her corner of the world. She knew that the man who had made her look more beautiful than even her bones could remember was there deep in the darkness beyond that boundary. It made her a little afraid to think of that.

Claude had been dead for fourteen years and, born as she was of a melancholy mother, her thoughts turned more often than she liked to the grave - to his grave - and to what lay within it. Her imagination, which had been troublingly active from childhood, had no problem conjuring the way his face would have been destroyed by the grave. She did not relish the idea of meeting that face somewhere in the darkness ahead of her. But she had always known that this night would come.

So she was here, and there was no help for it but to live a little longer and hope that the reunion was a joyous one. Perhaps, she thought, it would be best if she did as she had done on the day that she and Claude had first met, and initiate the conversation. She halted four or five strides from the trees and stared into the blackness.

"Husband?" she said.

-5-

. . .

Kirsty went to the cabinet. On the bottom shelf she found a hammer. The irony was not lost on her. As she gripped the handle, she spoke:

"There's a hammer here," she said. "Funny. I knew a woman who killed people with a hammer once. Years ago. It was the death of her."

Kirsty's grip upon the hammer's grainy, wooden handle tightened as a sudden realization came over her. The paintings. Their colors. The ineffable meanings hidden within. She saw with a terrible clarity just how stupid she had been. The golden hues and abstracted patterns had been carved into her psyche long ago and remained embedded in her soul, forever part of her. So deeply, in fact, that she had taken them for granted. But it was the image of the house that gave it away. The six gold and black pillars — between them a doorway leading to an inferno that blacked out the heavens; the house was a work of loving tribute to the infernal device. It was a shrine to the Lament Configuration. A current of shudders passed through Kirtsy's body. This house and everything in it was an agent of the Wastes.

No sooner had Kirsty made her realization than she heard the pistol's hammer click into place. Kirsty hung her head and cursed herself under her breath.

"Don't move," Walter said. "He'll be along shortly."

"Why?" Kirsty said without turning around.

"He wants to talk with you. Share his plans."

"No," Kirsty said. "Not that. Why have you done this to yourself? You've damned yourself. I'll never understand why people do it."

"Life is complicated, Mademoiselle. Maybe decisions do not come so easy for some as they do for others, such as yourself. So it becomes necessary to, I believe they say, hedge the bets."

"You're afraid you'll end up in Hell, so you make a deal with the Devil? That makes no sense."

"It is not for you to understand. It is not your path. You are there, and I am—"

Before he could finish his sentence, Kirsty twisted her body and hurled the hammer toward the man with the gun. His eyes widened and he pulled the trigger. Kirsty braced herself, heard first the click of the hammer striking the chamber. But instead of the report of a bullet being fired, she only heard a heavy thudding sound, like a wet cabbage hitting a brick wall. And then Walter was on the ground. She'd hit her mark.

"That's for bringing a gun to a hammer fight," Kirsty said.

Kirsty stood quickly, backing away from the man. But Walter remained still as she moved through the darkness of the room. Cautiously she went to his side. The glint of moonlight caught her eye and told her all she needed to know. There was blood, and it was streaming from Walter's head in freshets, spreading across the floor. She stepped over it and crouched down by his side. He wasn't breathing, partly because the hammer had struck him directly between the eyes, driving his nose into his brain, and partly because the man had likely died before he even hit the ground.

She grabbed the gun from his hand, pointed it at his bleeding body, and pulled the trigger just to be safe. The gun misfired for the second time. Kirsty examined the weapon in her hands and noticed just how old the piece of equipment truly was. It looked like something that had been used in the American Revolutionary War. The gun, and likely too its ammunition, were relics from a more prosperous time for The Devil's Island. Kirsty dropped the gun to the floor, picked up the blood-soaked hammer, and went outside. The darkness was intimidating. Though there were a few stars out tonight, they shed little light on the lawn and none whatsoever on the jungle beyond.

-6-

Kirsty set foot on the damp earth of the jungle, expecting the next portion of her journey to be far from uneventful. As the foliage thickened, the rain began in short bursts, and though the view before her was dark and more than a little disquieting, she was able to appreciate that the jungle did possess its own kind of eerie beauty. Stoic trees reached higher than her eyes could see, the animals that found their homes here sang their strange jungle songs, and on occasion showed themselves to the interloper who dared trespass through their domain. Catching fleeting glimpses of their bodies disappearing behind branches, trunks, and leaves, Kirsty was reminded of the Runner on Lodovico Street weaving between the withered trunks, and wondered if he wasn't here, now, watching her stumble her way blindly to her death.

Kirsty shook the thought from her mind and maintained her course, searching for any sign of Madame Rembert. Would the old woman be waiting for her with a weapon as Walter had been, or would she be surprised to see her alive, mistaken in the certainty that her errand boy had done her bidding and done it well? Kirsty certainly hoped to catch the old woman off guard. She wanted to see the look of surprise on the old cow's face. But rather than dwell on what lay ahead and let the fear of its unknown possibilities get the better of her, Kirsty kept her thoughts in the present: on the jungle, the slender path before her, and the soft earth beneath her feet.

It became harder and harder to focus, however, once she found a piece of Madame Rembert's clothing: a shoe, sticking out of the ground, its toe buried in the dirt as though the old woman had trod in quicksand and, in her haste, stepped out of the shoe and kept her pace, never once looking back for fear of some Fiend close at her back. As Kirsty journeyed on, she came across more and more articles of Madame Rembert's clothing: another shoe, her stockings, and then a shawl, blowing across the threshold of the jungle like an orphaned ghost seeking its new haunt.

She was passing beyond the jungle now. Dawn was hours in front of her, the last bit of sunlight hours behind. She was deep in the middle of her night, and knew that her journey had only just begun. As she walked on, curiosity and caution gave way to uncertainty and dread. The further she traveled, the darker the night seemed to grow. Forms in front of her blurred, their lines of definition defying Kirsty's eyes. Did she see another piece of clothing, or was that a plant? Overhead, was that a bird seeking a fresh carcass, or the last of the jungle's canopy waving her farewell?

She had prepared herself for a hard journey after putting down the man in the hotel. It was then that the rules of the game had changed, or rather, that she was again reminded of the game's distaste for predictability, and that the only rule was that the game ended when it had no more use for you. And yet, armed with this information, Kirsty was still unprepared for what came next. No matter how hard she tried to prepare for the worst, what came always surprised her.

The jungle opened up, and delivered Kirsty to the entrance of that infamous structure of stone and mortar: the hand-made Hell of the French government — the place of shame with the tiny cells where countless prisoners were housed, tortured, and eventually died all alone only to have their bodies thrown into a mass grave, and covered over by dirt and by time, their lives forgotten by history, their stories lost to the ages.

The prison of The Devil's Island was as terrible to Kirsty's eyes as anything she'd seen in the Wastes, and as she walked towards it, the earth beneath her feet grew noticeably damp, until she found herself struggling to keep her balance in an ever-thickening black mud. She walked on until she came upon Madame Rembert.

Kirsty halted suddenly. Madame Rembert stared up at her, the woman's eyes and mouth open wide in a silent shriek of terror. The woman's body, however, was nowhere to be seen. What lay in the mud was a sheaf of flesh — the skin of her face, from her forehead to her withered breasts — seemingly torn from her body in the midst of a despairing cry, or perhaps, Kirsty thought, martyred ecstasy. Whatever her state of mind at the time of her death (and dead she must be, for only now that Kirsty looked closer did she see that it wasn't water which made moist this earth, but the lifeblood of the old woman, surely spilled in its entirety), any questions to which Madame Rembert held the answers had been taken with her. Kirsty hoped the old woman had found her husband at last, and that reunited, their suffering was greater now than their love had been the last time they saw one another alive.

Kirsty moved ahead, entering the prison. As she did so, the clouds glided across the thin sliver of moon that hung in the sky, blotting out the last remaining fragment of light in the night sky. It astonished her that, after so many journeys into the heart of darkness, trying for thirty years to run from The Cold Man and his legacy in her life, she only ever seemed to find herself moving inexorably closer to him with every step.

-7-

The Big House was an illusion, which became truer the deeper Kirsty ventured. The two roofs above ground were facades: frames of weather-warped timber and weather-tattered canvas. But below ground, a real world lay waiting to be discovered. No, not world; worlds. On the first floor Kirsty found a maze of interconnected chambers, with something scrawled on every wall, seemingly by the same madman. At first, Kirsty thought it gibberish, but the closer she looked, the more the pattern began to emerge. Yes, there were calculations here, such as a man of science might have recognized. But the solutions were offered in far less conventional forms. In a recipe for jam, there were insights into the way an unborn soul might be taught to choose its own parents. In an analysis of pastel blue and its power to hypnotise, were found the encoded means of taking the life of any living being, and repurposing its life essence into another body.

On the floor below these chambers of science and madness was a furnace. But even further below, in the sub-basement, Kirsty found the end, and perhaps the beginning as well to both the flames and the fevers.

At the end of a long, dark, damp and ancient

concrete hallway was a doorway. The second Kirsty saw it, she knew it led to the Other Place.

Kirsty saw all of this, her mouth sealed shut in a grimace of resolve as she passed through the halls, as she made her way down into the lower chambers, and ultimately approached the two massive doors carved from stone. And reaching the end of one journey, but the beginning of another, she saw then that the doors were connected to an ancient system of weights and counterweights that caused them to open and close when pressed upon. As she moved in to more closely examine the device, unseen birds filled the passage between this world and the one she was knocking on, their panicked chirps echoing off the stone walls.

Just like the invisible birds that flew overhead, she could not see what lay on the other side with any clarity, but she could hear the sounds coming from Hell with horrible lucidity. There were screams, and sobbings, and prayers being offered to unholy things. The sounds made her stomach turn. Despite this, she reached for the lever to open the door. She was already past the point of no return. A man she'd never met had discovered her whereabouts and convinced her to forsake the safety of her hiding place for the epicenter of Hell's double doors. Kirsty wrapped her hand around the lever, realizing this could prove to be the greatest journey of her life, but would likely be her very undoing.

"Do you know what the word autopsy means?" asked a voice from within the darkness.

Kirsty wrenched her hand back from the lever as though it had burned her, and while skin pulled itself taut, gooseflesh spreading from head to toe, and back again. The voice came from somewhere behind her. *The* voice. She hadn't been in the presence of its owner in thirty years, and yet she still heard it almost every night in her dreams. But this was no dream. It was him. It was The Cold Man.

-8-

Her feet refused to move. Trembling, but not daring to turn around, she found she couldn't bring herself to answer the question the voice had posed. The fear in her was insurmountable. Had she been able to speak, however, she was uncertain she'd even be able to attempt to answer his question when so many of her own began to fight for first position; After three decades of running, why would any sane person turn and run into the fire? Could the Cold Man be killed? What were the odds this was all some terrible dream?

"For most people it's a death word." The voice said, invading her thoughts - stopping them in their tracks. "Mutilated corpses. Darkness. Incisions. But when the blinders of fear are stripped away, only one thing remains: seeing. It's time to open the door. That which lays on the other side has been waiting for you."

In front of her, the two doors seemed to beg for the Cold Man's request to be heeded. She wanted to scream. Instead, again she reached for the lever, hand shaking. This time, she pulled it. With incremental movement, the doors slid open, but nothing revealed itself from that crack between worlds. Blackness, thick as the wall Madame Rembert had pointed to, was all that Kirsty could see at first.

When there was enough room to squeeze through into the next world, however, Kirsty did so, moving past the chaotic racket of unseen birds and into the

Wastes that marked the dividing line of this infernal nowhere. With one foot on earth, and one in Hell, the Wastes opened before her.

How often she'd thought of this place, since the moment when she first encountered the term in a book about the topography of Hell. It had been, as she remembered, a somewhat condescending book, mocking the fact that those who spoke of infernal regions constantly contradicted each other and themselves. Kirsty would have gained some satisfaction from taking the smug ones by their collars and showing them what she saw now.

Her sight seemed both wider and higher than it had ever been before, as though the bone of her skull had surrendered to the ambition of her new vision, and retreated. Though her sight was not the only sense that had new appetite; her ears not only heard with new clarity, but when the wind here blew against her face she could have named the origin of every note that grazed her skin. It was the smell of the Wastes, however, that moved her most deeply. She had read just days before that it was in humanity's sense of smell where the greatest repository of associations and memories lay.

It was from the smell alone that Kirsty guessed this place had earned it name. But even without the smell, the Wastes lived up to its name. Greasy mud was all she could see for a hundred feet in front of her. Beyond that, the vista seemed to stretch out for miles with nary a topographical distinction to break up the monotonous view. This piece of Hell was impressive in its banality. There was nothing worthy of mockery here. It seemed a place perfectly suited as a punishment. It was in the middle distance, however, that Kirsty saw why the Cold Man had brought her here. There, she caught sight of a teeming mass of bodies gathered around a large and ancient-looking stone well; it was the only variation in her entire field of vision.

"Do you see?" The Cold Man said. "This is what they do to pay their respects to the great Absence which is God. Above or Below, it makes no difference. God is a well with no water to which pilgrims who are already damned come to drink. This is the void gazing at the void. This is the place where I realized I am nothing, nor ever was, and as a result, I decided to finally expose the charade."

Kirsty perceived the significance of The Cold Man's delivery, but the message was lost on her. She dared a backward glance in his direction and felt her blood freeze in her veins at the sight of him. The Cold Man stood there, exactly as she remembered him. His skin was white as porcelain, his shorn head carved with lines that crisscrossed his face and head. Where the lines met, thick, rusted nails had been driven deep into scalp and bone. If these wounds had ever caused him to bleed, that day had long since passed. The exposed flesh beneath the surface was grey like old meat. The most striking things of all, though, were the demon's eyes. They were two portals that transported her to that place on Lodovico Street and reduced her to her basest, feral fears. The two orbs in his noble skull were black as the night, with a silvery glint, and contained only the sentiment of decay.

She said nothing.

"I am gathering many magics," he said. "All I have need of now are my disciples. Your presence is requested. I have cast my first witness. A detective. You will be my second. You will witness my great working from your throne on earth, and the detective shall witness my ascension below."

. . .

-9-

"Why?" was the only word that escaped her mouth.

"Most who cross my path are not fortunate enough to escape with breath in their body. You and the detective have this rare honor in common."

She looked at him curiously. Her throat was dry. She wanted to ask him more questions. She wanted to tell him to go fuck himself. She wanted to scream the name "Pinhead" at him. Before she could do any of these things, he spoke again. Instead, she said nothing.

The Cold Man looked at her curiously. "Are you afraid? Where is the bravery? The anger? The rebellious spirit from the girl on Lodovico Street?"

"I can't help you." A tear rolled down her cheek.

"You will. I have left nothing to chance. Should I fail, there is another who will rise in my place. I have spread my seed that my legacy may live on. She is in your world, moving amongst the living, even as we speak."

Kirsty looked at him with eyes wide. He was a father? How could God have allowed it?

"Look at the lost souls," he said. "This is it. The End of All Things."

Kirsty maintained her gaze, staring at The Cold Man. At his eyes. Those eyes. The eyes of the creature that ruined her life.

"Look!" he snapped.

Kirsty flinched at the Cold Man's outburst. She did as she was told, and looked round slowly. The Cold Man was right. The many tens of thousands of pilgrims were assembled around a hole, which she deemed in her mind the Well of the Wastes. A hole. A great big hole. As she watched, a column of young mothers carrying their babes naked in their arms walked purposefully towards the hole, like devout Catholics coming to an altar to give thanks. Their feet did not falter, even for an instant. They kept walking, until there was no more ground. Clutching their infants, they went over the edge, one after the other.

"My God," she said.

"'*Jesus wept*' is more appropriate, is it not?" he said.

Was he mocking her? Did he know the importance of those words? They were the last that Frank Cotton ever spoke to her. It was as if The Cold Man had always been watching. Remembering. Waiting for the perfect time to use them against her.

"And if He weeps for your pain, why not heal it?" the Cold Man said. "If He wishes you were not so weak and easily tempted, why not give you strength? If He hears your cries, why is He silent?"

The Cold Man laid his palm upon her spine, close to her neck. She felt a barbed blossom of ice spread across her back. Her teeth began to chatter. Her heart thumped against her rib cage as though it were trying to escape her body, which was still in shock from the Cold Man's touch. Kirsty wished for distance from this place, for safety from this demon, for the possibility of feeling any recollection other than terror. Kirsty's mind retreated. Time became a lie, and sound an elegy. But the smell...oh God the smell. It called Kirsty back from her depths. It breached her icy fugue, waking her mind once more.

"Agree," he said. "And you will witness the conquering of Heaven and Hell."

Kirsty had tears welling in her eyes. "I... don't think—"

"I didn't bring you here to think!"

He came at Kirsty suddenly, and delivered a

vicious blow that threw her down in the dirt. The dust that she tried to hawk up had the foul taste of old shit. She spat, but the stink or the taste, or both, could not be expelled.

"This is not what I desire," the Cold Man said. "You were exquisite. You were a force. You were worthy." He looked away from her, glancing up at the hordes. "You should die if you cannot be who you were."

"I'm sorry," Kirsty lied. As she spoke, she spit out more of the foul-tasting dirt.

"Now is not the time for apologies. If you wait any longer, it will all be over. An opportunity that comes along once in a millennia will have come and gone. There is nothing here of the witness I desire."

The Cold Man continued to stare into the distance as he spoke. Kirsty, on the ground, saw the gleam of the claw-headed hammer in the corner of her eye. In her fear, she had forgotten she'd brought her weapon with her. It lay now in the dirt, mere inches from her grasp.

"Have you made your choice?" he said.

"I...," she said, looking back at him. She saw that his eyes remained focused on the worshipers as they bowed down to their great hole. The Cold Man's message was clear. Her cowardice was beneath him, in all regards, and he would only grace her with his visage when she had made her decision. In that moment, her hand darted into the dirt, and she drew the hammer close to the small of her back.

"There is no time left now," he said. "We have played out all the puzzles."

"This is a puzzle to you," she said, summoning the courage to utter the next word: "Pinhead?"

At this, The Cold Man's steely gaze moved finally from the throng to Kirsty, the flecks of silver in his bleak, blank eyes rising with his anger. Behind her back, Kirsty squeezed the handle of the hammer, her knuckles white with rage.

"You dare use that word," he said.

There was a tremor in his voice that belied his stoicism. Had she hurt his feelings? She couldn't allow herself to believe it was possible. Just another of the Devil's tricks. If for a moment she permitted any idea claiming otherwise — if for a second she thought she had the upper hand — the battle, she knew, would be lost.

Then he was leaning down in front of her. She willed herself to remain in place as he brought his pallid flesh close enough to suck the warmth from her, his carrion breath stinking worse than the shit-stained soil.

"With that remark, you have chosen death," he told her.

She looked at the creature that kneeled in front of her. He was regarding her with abject hatred and she saw, for the first time, that she had been wrong; the demon was not exactly as she'd remembered him. Though ageless, he had grown older, and wearier. Kirsty saw despair and fatigue in his eyes. Where once a genius had shone, there was now only desolation. In a different life, she might have felt pity for this odious beast, but this was not that life, nor would it ever be.

"If you have nothing left to say, then make peace with your chosen fiction."

"I want to say something," Kirsty said, near breathless.

"Say it."

"I found your tell."

At that, Kirsty loosed a cry of hatred, and with her concealed hand she brought the hammer out of hiding and swung it, claw first, at the Demon's head. It connected with his cheek, the sound of metal grinding against bone. The demon staggered backward and a nail caught in the hammer's claw, and wrenched sideways. The Cold Man uttered a guttural cry of anguish as a beam of harsh blue light burst forth from the wound in his face.

-10-

Kirsty was on her feet in an instant and launched herself toward the doorway that led back to the island.

The Cold Man screamed in fury, and before Kirsty could reach the doorway, he was on her, flinging her back into the soiled mire of the Wastes. He was in pursuit, his objective plain: to end her existence.

He struck at her, his blows a fury, opening wounds on her face and neck. For a split second, Kirsty saw a vision of Frank Cotton wearing his brother's flesh, standing above her in the attic on Lodovico Street, possessed of a similar rage and similar intent, a furious tattoo of lashings gouging her flesh. The weight of the memories begged her to lose consciousness. It would be so easy to let go. She would be free. She felt her life slipping away and with it, her fear. She felt something else in her haze, but couldn't find the words to describe the sensation. It was a heaviness, not of spirit, but one that remained in the physical world. It weighted her hand down.

She focused her attention on the heaviness. It felt important to her, as though it were trying to tell her something, as though it held some significance. It brought her back to the house on Lodovico Street, and the woman who ruined everything.

Julia.

She had murdered all those innocent men.

With her hammer.

Like the one Kirsty still gripped in her hand.

It was the weapon that had launched this assault.

Kirsty's consciousness stirred in her, surprised to find that her body still gripped the hammer.

Without thinking, Kirsty swung the hammer. It connected a moment later, driving more metal into bone. But as Kirsty pulled the hammer back, intent to strike The Cold Man once more, the hammer's claw took with it a nail embedded in the Demon's nose. He let out a curse as another, brighter shaft of corrupted light oozed from the fresh wounds in his face. He instantly released his grip on her and stepped back as he attempted to block the light that now poured from his wounds.

Kirsty could breathe again.

She opened her eyes, regaining her bearings. There she saw the Cold Man, staring at her. His fury was subsiding, giving way to something else. Though she could not tell what it was.

He made no advance towards her. Moving only on instinct now, she crawled a few paces back, lest he decide to make another appeal. She stood then, and reeled for a moment, afraid that her legs would give out on her. Her mind suddenly took her back to grade school. To that classroom where the wretched Miss Pryor had struck Kirsty when she'd caught her teacher in a lie. She had never finished the assignment. Kirsty's trip to the nurse's office saw to that. But all these years later, Kirsty finally knew what she would ask for mankind.

Before the Cold Man had ever entered her life,

Kirsty had already learned to stop asking things of God. Miss Pryor was far from a great teacher, but that didn't mean Kirsty hadn't learned any lessons from the woman. And now, in this place, when Kirsty felt the furthest from God that she'd ever felt in her life, she knew what she wanted of Him - and she wanted it for her and for the good of all Mankind: to be rid of the blight that was the Cold Man. Perhaps he had once served some purpose, but that purpose had long since played out and what was left was an angry husk of rage and sorrows.

I know better than to ask you for anything, Kirsty thought, directing her appeal heavenward. *But I'm willing to make an exception. Even if I don't survive this, please don't let this sack of shit keep doing this to people.*

Then, as if in answer, she felt a kind of ecstasy begin to course through her. She felt herself come alive. She wanted to live. She wanted — finally — to live. The feeling began in the fingertips of the hand which gripped the hammer - a newfound vitality threading itself up her arm, under her skin, into bone. She understood her enemy in that moment; realized the pleasure in his pain. Though he was an agent of Hell, that Hell was of his own design. And in that moment, she knew one thing: as certainly as she'd seen the deeper soul — or what was left of the soul — in her adversary, he too witnessed a depth in her previously unseen. She didn't wait for him to confirm what she already knew. Instead, she began to move toward the doorway.

"You won't follow me, you son of a bitch," she told him with her remembered courage.

"There she is," the Cold Man replied, still unmoving, but slowly smiling. "And taking a piece of me with her. This is, to some, a romance."

"Don't make this something it isn't. We both lost

something in this fight. I see you now. You had me fooled that your cowardice is actually righteous anger. But you're just a bully, afraid of being seen. That's all you've ever been."

As she spoke, Kirsty edged closer to the door. All the while the Cold Man stared at her with a curious mix of obvious contempt, and what also seemed to be admiration.

"You are welcome to your trophy," he said. "In the world that is to come, it will be priceless."

"Why don't we just wait and see how everything shakes out. A lot of apocalypses have been predicted. Last I counted, none of them have ever happened."

"Then you haven't been paying attention."

"I'll keep my eyes open," she said.

And then she was out of the door at a run - out of the Devil's world and back on his island. But before the world at her back was gone forever, she heard the Cold Man's voice calling to her one last time.

"Do keep them open, Kirsty. I *will* come for you."

-11-

I survived, Kirsty thought. *How did I survive again, where so many others have failed?*

It was a question that had plagued her most of her adult life. She didn't want to believe that something bonded her to the darkness. But the darkness that continued to follow her, like an umbilicus never properly severed, seemed an inextricable part of her, albeit one that should not remain. But remain it would. Kirsty understood that more with each passing day. And now, as if serving to remind her, the doorway through which she had entered the Wastes was beginning to refashion itself before her very eyes.

She looked down the tunnel, toward the stairs that would lead her out of this hellish prison, but her feet refused to move. Her gaze returned to the doorway, which continued its transformation, the mortar and mechanics disappearing into the concrete halls of the prison's basement completely. The doorway and its parts didn't fade from sight, like some spectral figure — they simply became one with the building, like an iron door welded shut, forever sealed, no longer functional. She was happy about the transformation. Though she now carried with her more memories of the infernal and what it wrought upon the human psyche, the sealed doorway had the benefit of safety, or at least the façade thereof.

When the door at last sealed itself shut, Kirsty left the passageway in the basement of the prison, passed through the halls of the Big House and found her way outside once more with little memory of how she had arrived there. The first rays of morning sunlight dappled the landscape as it broke through the trees, causing the jungle at the threshold of the prison to appear brighter than she'd expected, as though she'd forgotten she might ever see the sun again. She found her footprints and followed them into the brush, never once relinquishing her grasp on the hammer, until she was in sight of the hotel. The old building was also a surprise to her eyes, as though she were viewing it with a new pair of eyes. In many ways, she was. She had followed hew own footsteps, which were essentially those of a dead woman — evidence of a former self, like a song sung by a long-dead crooner — and they led her to a hotel she had once thought charming. But where she had seen style and character, she now only saw the warped, worn walls of a building that seemed to be sinking into the earth, as though Hell itself was trying to reclaim it. This place had nothing left to show her. She turned her eyes from it and went to the dock where she flagged down the ship which she'd paid to wait for her.

"If you don't see me on that dock in thirty-six hours," Kirsty had said, "you're free to go back home. And if I don't return, neither should you. Kiss your loved ones and pray for a tomorrow."

She had doubted the captain's promise to wait for her. Had she any tears left, she would have cried at the sight of the vessel. Instead, she stood on the shore, hammer in hand, sun searing her wan flesh, watching as the black boat was deployed and came for her. She never took her eyes off the boat.

By the time it reached her, the sun was at her back and it was growing dark again. Silently, she climbed into the boat without any problems. Then the two oarsmen, careful not to question the woman with the blood-soaked hammer, pushed the boat back into the ocean and rowed toward the reddening horizon until they reached the ship. From there, Kirsty would take a train and two planes, and she'd be back on her own continent within another twenty-four hours.

That was the extent to which she was willing to plan ahead. The tasks of finding a new home, again, and starting life over, again, were simply too daunting a proposition. And though she knew they were the twin realities with which she was presently faced, she was content to focus on the island that grew smaller and smaller at her back with each of the oarsmen's thrusts.

I'm not afraid of storms, for I'm learning how
to sail my ship.

— LOUISA MAY ALCOTT

THE TOLL -
EPILOGUE

-1-

Kirsty settled into her new life with an ease that troubled her. The first call she made when she established a secure phone line was to the supposed Dr. Lansing. Kirsty was not surprised when the number led to a deli in New York. Kirsty was even less surprised when the man who answered the phone — he called himself Hans — stated that he'd never heard of a Dr. Lansing and as far as he knew, the number she called had always belonged to his deli. She thanked him for his time. He hung up the phone, wishing her a good day with a single word: "Gesundheit."

Certain that any road to reach the man calling himself Dr. Lansing, if man he was, would lead to nowhere, Kirsty changed course and followed currents of information that were in the air. Once she knew what to look for, the information flowed all too quickly. Something big had been happening in the world, and then beyond. There were stories of mass slaughter of the world's most powerful magicians, some deaths indescribably violent, and in one case where the man had been found with his stomach pulled out through his asshole, seemingly personal or at least done with a notable appetite for suffering.

But the accounts didn't stop there. In New York people had reported seeing doorways to other worlds, and faceless demons with raging hard-ons walking empty streets in the dead of night. In Arizona, a world-famous televangelist was left for dead in the scorching heat in the very same city that a family sought vengeance on the man who murdered their children and several others.

And then there were the rumors that the Wastes and everything associated with it had vanished overnight without a trace. Kirsty heard rumors that demons were summoned by devices and that those demons failed to appear, when the devices opened portals into sheer nothingness, and that Lucifer himself had abandoned his post and was walking the planet, waiting. For what, she knew not, but the implications robbed her of what little sleep she would normally find.

In her searches, however, two words remained constant: Harry D'Amour, the name of a detective living in New York. This she knew to be the other witness the Cold Man had mentioned. Kirsty resisted the urge to call this detective. She had far more pressing matters to address, and she couldn't risk exposing herself again before she had done what needed doing.

-2-

. . .

Months after her encounter with the Cold Man on the aptly named Devil's Island, Kirsty lay awake in bed, the sun long since set, the information she'd gleaned swimming through her mind while the mockingbirds sounded their warnings, mirroring the alarms going off inside her head.

There was so much work to be done; her great work. Every night since last she saw the Cold Man, she expected him to appear. She imagined all the ways he would drag her back to the Wastes and throw her into the well, to be united with the God that never existed. But the Cold Man never came. And instead Kirsty replayed the events that transpired on the Devil's Island over and again.

Something the Cold Man had said to her that day had stayed with her.

There is another, he had said. He had revealed that he had spread his seed and that it - *she* - was in the world. Kirsty had followed the trails in the sand and entertained the rumors as far as they would take her, but every current of information she had gleaned on her own had reached a dead end. Every current, save for the one the Cold Man had supplied for her himself.

Knowing what to look for, it wasn't long before she had in her hands a police report detailing the brutal murders of four university professors that took place shortly before her visit from the Cold Man. Kirsty recognized the names as belonging to four of the world's most powerful magicians. It was too coincidental to be ignored.

These unlucky four had been butchered, strung up, flayed, and mangled beyond all recognition. There was language in the report suggesting a theory that at least three other people (one an infant, based on the bloody hand and knee-prints indicating a crawling babe) had been present during the time of the massacre, but that no trace of their whereabouts had ever been found. It was as though they had vanished into thin air.

Kirsty knew how easy it was for people to vanish, especially when the passages that spirited them away could only be opened from one side. But, no matter how canny, it is impossible for a stranger in a strange land to go unnoticed forever. Kirsty had watched for the signs that eventually wound their way back to her. And her vigilance had paid off. As she suspected, Hell found its way back to her. It always did.

And now, as Kirsty turned over in bed, willing herself to stay down for a few more hours, her mind went to tomorrow. She had an appointment with Death's Daughter when the sun reared its ugly head, and she'd need her energy for what was to come. Did the creature know about her? Kirsty couldn't say, but in the same way the Infernal's agents always seemed drawn to her, she suspected she was doing her part to remain drawn to the Infernal's agents. That was the thing about Hell. Despite its existence or recent supposed lack thereof, it would be in her always. She could not imagine life without it. Wherever her crusades delivered her, she would bring with her the images, and knowledge, and losses that had delivered her to such places. But she would never let them stop her.

As Kirsty clutched her pillow close, wondering when she would at last be done with this game, her eyes went to the nightstand upon which the Cold Man's nail sat in a mason jar, reminding her of one hard truth: it didn't matter what she asked of God, for even if Hell had never existed, mankind would always be there to fashion one for itself.

. . .

THE END

NESTING

I

This is a confession.

I had a terrible accident a few months ago. It's not easy for me to talk about.

I remember driving. It was raining so hard, I thought the sky might have broken open. Driving in the rain had always made me nervous. This only made it worse. And my heart was racing. Then I remember bright headlights flashing. There was a horn, too, I think. And the next thing I know, I'm waking up in the hospital with a big tube in my stomach.

A truck had blasted through a busy intersection and hit my tiny peanut of a car. This big fucking truck, going about its day, plowed right into me. My car flipped over. Twice. Then spun around a few times like the dial on a combination lock. I woke up with tons of cuts, scrapes, bruises and scratches. Those all happened at the time of the accident, of course. But I guess that's obvious. I just don't remember that part, so I feel like I have to say it. First I'm looking at flashing lights, and then I'm lying in a hospital bed feeling like my mind is in a million fractured pieces, buried under a layer of soggy cotton, like a bottle of fish oil pills left out in the sun too long.

When I woke up, there were doctors standing over me like a scene out of a bad soap opera. They all started talking in slow motion. And I remember feeling my heart start to race again. It wasn't because of what they were saying, though. I could barely comprehend the words as I pulled myself from the murky depths of wherever I'd been. My heart was galloping in my chest because I had lost time. I didn't know if I'd been in this room for three hours or three years.

I asked for a mirror. The goddamn doctors did what men always do and started to soften the blow by letting me know that the important thing was that I was alive. It was like all those times I'd heard how beautiful I was if I criticized a part of my body. I fucking hate this. I don't need the big strong man's affection or approval. I once asked a digital artist to show me what my hair would look like if I cut it off and dyed it black. Instead of giving me the service he advertised, he came back at me with some trite condescension about me being pretty exactly as I was. What the fuck does that have to do with anything? And *that* was exactly what was happening as the doctors handed me the mirror. I didn't care about how third degree burns healed, or the advancements in keloid scar removal surgery. I didn't ask about that. I just wanted a fucking mirror. Not a knight in shining armor.

I ignored their misguided goodwill gestures and stared into the cheap pastel pink hand mirror they'd given me. What I saw took my breath away. I looked like a moldy cantaloupe wrapped in gauze. As I examined my new face, the doctors again reminded me how lucky I was for various reasons, and that I'd also broken my right leg and three ribs. But they saved the best for last.

I feel like I should have been more concerned, but even though my face was all but unrecognizable, the only thing I could think about was the smell. Not my own, though. I'm talking about that horrible, sickly sweet hospital smell. You know, the sticky-feeling stench that gets up in your nose and behind your throat? The one that smells like cough drops and burning rubber? Well, sitting there, looking at my disfigurements, listening to the litany of damages to my body, and how fortunate I was to have had them instead of myriad others, that awful smell was the only thing that bothered me.

I didn't care that I'd have scars. I was never a bikini girl anyway. Before the accident I was always told I was beautiful. I never paid much attention to it. Of course when I look at old pictures of me now, I see that they were right. But, honestly, the face that stares at me from the mirror these days – the face that first stared at me the day I woke up in the hospital - is the face that feels, somehow, right. You probably think I'm insane for saying that. But if you're already thinking that, you might not want to read the rest of this. My hang-ups are the least of your worries. Just like those thoughtful doctors, I'm saving the best part for last. You see, after hemming and hawing, they finally told me that I'd undergone an emergency hysterectomy while I was unconscious. Something about a puncture and the bruising on my spine. I don't know. I stopped paying attention because the reason didn't matter. All I knew then was that a feeling of distinct relief passed through me. It was like a pressure valve had been released.

I swear to God, for as long as I could remember people would ask me awful questions like, 'did I have anyone special in my life', or 'when was I finally going to have my first kid', implying that I should begin work on my litter now. All these stupid fucking intrusions that were nobody's business. But just like that, I was freed from having to answer them. So a ripple flowed over and through my body because now I had the mother of all get-out clauses. What's funny is that I never really thought about it. I'd always just instinctually danced around the questions.

"Some day!" I'd say, but it wasn't until that very moment that I realized 'd never planned on having any kids at all.

I just never felt maternal. I had never liked kids. And babies had always creeped me out. They just seemed so squirmy, and squishy, and wet all the time. It never made sense to me why would anybody want to deal with that all day, every day.

And of course, in typical fashion, the doctors also reassured me that they had done everything they could. I honestly think they have to say that. It's such a cliché, isn't it? It's like someone saying 'rise and shine'. I don't think they actually mean it. Why do you want me to wake up and be cheery? What the fuck do you care? They probably don't even realize what they're saying. It's like it's something that's coming out of their mouths at a certain time of the day; like cocks crowing at the sunrise.

It's the morning. Rise and shine.

Your uterus is gone. We did everything we could.

It didn't matter how hard they tried. Why bother wasting more time? It was gone. And I didn't care. I just wanted to rinse the hospital smell out of my nose.

Then the doctors left and I stayed there for *seven*

more days. I watched the pinkish fluid come out of the tube in my stomach. Nurses helped me out of bed and put me in a wheelchair when I wanted to use the bathroom. A lot of people tried to visit, but I told the hospital staff I didn't want to see anyone. I barely wanted to eat, and that had nothing to do with the hospital food. Only one thing there had any appeal, but not for any reason that was immediately clear. Somewhere along the line, for some reason, I developed a voracious appetite for stale meat. Not spoiled meat, mind you. Dry meat. Hard meat. Luckily, hospital meat is comparable to sawdust, and I loved it. One time I left my room, found a vending machine and bought all the beef jerky it had in it. That night, lying in my bed, I ate four bags, and I was happier than I'd been in months. Just me and my jerky. Or so I thought.

Finally, I got to go home.

I still hadn't seen any friends or family since the accident, and rather than bother with any of that noise, I just had the hospital call me a cab. It had been nearly a month since I had last set foot in my home. Before that, my life had been pretty uneventful. I don't think the accident fucked my head up. But sometimes I do have to wonder; maybe it was the accident, or maybe it was the hospital. All I know is that I hadn't been home in twenty-one days.

I left my apartment by myself and got into the worst accident of my life.

When I returned three weeks later, I wasn't alone.

• • •

II

It took a little while for me to figure this out, mind you. It started with a general feeling of wanting a change. I don't live an extravagant life. My apartment is small. Just a one bedroom on the second floor of a Spanish colonial building. The kind that are everywhere in Los Angeles. I passed a dozen just like mine on my way home, and I swear I thought the cab driver was going to stop at all of them.

At first I wondered if I had hit my head too hard. Something had to be wrong with my recognition. But when the driver pulled up to the curb of my building in broad daylight, it was like I was seeing it through new eyes. Nothing set it apart from the rest of the pink-tiled buildings that lined the block. Walking to my door and sticking the key in, I half expected someone to open it from within and ask me who I was and what the hell I thought I was doing. But the key fit the lock, and the door swung open without anyone protesting.

When I walked in, it was like entering a stranger's house. I felt no connection to the objects in there. The photos held no significance. The furniture disgusted me. The feng shui was way off, and it bothered me to my core. Who was the person who had lived in this place, and how could she have had such awful taste? Worst of all was the bedroom. I couldn't even bring myself to cross the threshold. I simply stared into the room, knowing I would never sleep in there again; and that everything had to go.

So I had a sale. I created signs, and put them all over the neighborhood, then opened my doors. Bargain hunters and lookie-loos came in droves. I didn't care how low they wanted to go. I sold everything that wasn't nailed down to the first bidder. If you wanted it and you had a way to get it out, it was yours.

By the time the sun had set, my apartment had been stripped bare. I sold it all. The furniture, the silverware, even the refrigerator. I didn't need it anyway. You'd have to be crazy to refrigerate beef jerky, right?

So with my walls bare, I started over. I went to some furniture stores, and department stores, and markets. I didn't buy anything for a few days, though. Nothing felt right. I didn't know exactly what I wanted or needed. I just knew that I'd find it eventually. And it took some time before I bought my first new trinket for my brand new life. I was walking through that big red store that every woman loves – and I'm no exception – when I saw it. I dropped the handheld basket to the ground, crossed from the cold tile floor to the carpeted square where the display had been erected, reached out my trembling hand, and plucked the fuzzy little stuffed lamb from the shelf. It was pure perfection. Its soft innocence was almost heartbreaking. I took it home and placed it on the bare floorboards of the bedroom in my apartment.

The rest of it all came pretty quickly after that, as though my lamb was the spark that ignited a great fire. I bought dressers, bedsheets, a small mattress, a thermometer, blankets, washcloths, bowls and spoons, a night light, bottles, a little rubber bathtub, and then finally, a crib. Even the least observant kind of person would be able to recognize a pattern here. But I didn't see it. Before the crib, I had purchased all of these things in bits and pieces, and when I arranged everything in the bedroom, I stood back and finally saw it for what it was, almost as though I had been putting a puzzle together without looking at the picture on the box. Well, I had finally assembled enough pieces to see it. It was a nursery.

It was also a complete surprise, but it made the rest of the shopping easier. So I bought the crib and everything else that goes along with that. I couldn't ignore it anymore. I couldn't even shrug it off as hysterics brought on by a past trauma. At least that would have actually made sense to people. This, though? How would I explain this?

But I want you to know that there *is* a pattern here. There *is* a strange kind of sense to it all. Think about this logically. Where does every person come from? One place, right? There's really only one way that every mammal on this planet enters this world. Through a female body. They gestate, they grow, and when it's time, they emerge. They go from being *there*, to being *here*. By that regard, our bodies are doorways.

And even though I couldn't bring any humans into this world, I guess it didn't necessarily mean that nothing could ever enter this world through my door.

III

It's been thirty-seven weeks since I left the hospital.

If you've read all the pregnancy books out there – and believe me, there are a lot of them! – you'll learn that when your baby starts to grow and move, at first it feels almost like carbonation; like tiny bubbles fizzing up inside you. I only learned that from reading the literature, though. I've never felt the bubbles, but I *do* feel things. That's why I picked up the books in the first place, and not one of them mentioned the feeling of a long, thick, razor blade running up and down the inside of your abdomen, like a tree branch in a low wind scraping against your bedroom wall.

I know every mammal comes at different times, but I don't think it's about what's coming out. I think it's about who it's coming out of. And it seems that no matter where you're coming form, or what you are, if you're entering this world through a woman, it's going to take about forty weeks. That's if you don't want any complications, of course.

I can tell you that not knowing when I conceived has had its disadvantages, but regardless of the date, I now know I'm out of the danger zone in terms of delivery. What I don't know is how I got so lucky.

I never even ended up showing. I have so much to be thankful for. No pesky questions. No discomfort. And most importantly, a healthy baby. There's been no more rewarding feeling in my life than the slow steady increase in her strength. She's pushing very hard these days. She's definitely ready. Funny thing is, I'm ready too. I'm ready for her to be here. And I'm ready to tell you everything.

As I said when I started, this is confession. And I haven't lied about anything. I just haven't told you all of it yet. Before you accuse me of not being fair, you have to remember that it's my story. I have to tell it the only way I know how. And I almost didn't want to tell it at all. It's not in my nature. But, since she's coming, it'll be your story very soon, so I feel like I have to share this. Especially because I don't think I'll be here to see the rest of it told.

The thing about my baby girl is that she's not so little. I told you I can feel her when she knocks on my tummy. And what I can feel is she's bigger than I am. A lot bigger. I don't mean it metaphorically, like, "hey, my love for you is larger than my own sense of being." I mean literally. Some people call them kicks. Pregnant moms might see a little foot, or a shoulder quickly repositioning itself. When I look down, sometimes it looks like the business end of a shovel is trying to dig its way out of my body from the inside out. So, like I said, I don't expect to be around much longer. But that's okay.

I used to live in fear. And I was so terrified of the fear, that I felt I just had to put an end to it. And that brings me to my accident, which wasn't strictly accidental. I'm embarrassed to admit that I was the one who ran the red light. I saw the truck, and I just thought it would be the fastest way to stop the fear. Everything else was true. The flashing lights. Waking up. The doctors condescending me.

But I do have one memory that sits somewhere within those events, but also exists outside of them as well, if that's possible. One piece of the puzzle that I didn't share with you. After the accident, and before waking up in the hospital, I met someone. The best way I can explain it is that I think I unlocked a kind of key. I don't exactly know how. It just feels like it was made up of the right ingredients, both organic and manufactured. Despair. Longing. Hatred. Fear. Violence. Transgression. And one hell of a two ton backwards somersault. Throw all of those against the back of my skull like ground meat and eggs in a mixing bowl and you've somehow got yourself a door to another world.

Before the accident, I was afraid all the time. Afraid of dying, ironically. But that fear can grow so strong that it gets to be too much and the pain of living outweighs the fear of not. Or the fear of naught. Either way, when I went away - during the time between the collision and the doctors' speeches – I was visited by a man, of sorts.

He was dressed in all black garments that made him look like a priest and a butcher rolled into one. His face was comprised of flesh, and gears, commingled. And his skin was too tight. Smooth. As though someone had left an animal hide in the sun too long. But he was beautiful. He held me in his arms. He told me I was important. That I had purpose. We danced, but we didn't use our bodies.

He showed me his world, which was austere and immense. It thrived on order, and I saw that everything was about perception. One person's trash was another person's treasure. One person's hell was another person's heaven. It was rapture. Not to sound too cliché, but being there felt like eternity wrapped in a single moment. And then he told me it was time I left, but before I did, he needed to know if I wanted to seal the door forever, or if I wanted to leave it open. The choice was mine. Things were moving so fast, then, but as his world receded before my eyes, I held my arm out and said only one word:

"Open."

Then he was gone and I was awake, and just before the stench of the hospital hit me, I could still smell the faintest traces of musk, leather, and black oil.

Now at some point, you may have found yourself asking, "why the crib?" Obviously she's not going to fit in it. I know this. I believe it's more of what psychologists would call a tribute. Think of it as a muscle memory exercise that prepares your mind and body for something. Sometimes it's to remember to maintain a certain mindset, or to avoid prior triggers in life. I think in this case it was my way of helping my body prepare for what's to come. After all, the woman with her legs in the air who has just conceived is a different woman entirely than the one who enters her hospital room 40 weeks later. And in the same way, I'm a different woman than the one who wanted to end it all nine months ago. I bought the things and I arranged them in the way a mother would. I stepped back and felt the knowledge of the life forming in my body – or, somehow, *beyond* my body. And now, all these months later, I'm ready.

Honestly, I thought the time in the austere world with my clockwork butcher was a dream at first. A more clinical mind might call it a subconscious manifestation of manufactured order brought on by shock, to make sense of a world that I only understood as chaos. But it's simply not true. It wasn't until I knew about *her*, that I understood about *him*. He's real. And she's real. Which means that places other than here are real. And that's the reason I'm not afraid for the next part anymore.

It's funny how I never thought I had a maternal bone in my body, until slowly all of those motherly instincts kicked in. I already know that my girl will be the most special thing in this world. But I think I have more reason than most to think so.

I can't wait for you all to meet her. I just wish I could see it happen.

THE DIVE

I swear to God you're not going to believe this story.

Let's just get that out of the way right at the beginning. But I promise that every word is true. I think. I mean, I can't be certain because, well, you'll see. It's all just too crazy. I don't know. Maybe I made it all up and I'm not actually sitting down at my desk typing anything. Maybe I'm strapped to a bed in a psych ward somewhere on a Thorazine drip telling myself a story about writing a story I made up to begin with. Wouldn't that be fucked? Though it *would* make more sense.

As they say, let's begin at the beginning. I had this job that sucked. It's not really groundbreaking material. This is one of those stories you might be able to call 'relatable.'

Shitty job. Fish in a barrel. Like a pop song. In music, all you have to do is throw in some bullshit about 'letting it all go on the weekend,' or 'being in a big city,' or 'just plain falling in love' and you've got yourself the ingredients for a number one single.

I've got an inkling this, too, is relatable, though I'm fairly sure that the part about me hating my job will be where the relatable aspects stop. And I'll let you know in advance that nobody falls in love. The good news is that even if this story is all in my head, at least I'll never know for sure!

As I was saying, my job was donkey balls. And I knew in my heart that I was wasting my life, and my potential. Sure, the money was good, and other than the long hours, I didn't really have any complaints. Sure, the gig was boring as hell, and made relationships tough because by the time I got off work, everyone else had already gone to bed. And sure, my boss was a dumbass who didn't deserve the gig. But I lived well. All my basic needs were met. I even had enough free time to explore other interests, but I wanted more! Nay, I was owed more! Some would call me lucky and tell me to shut my fucking mouth. I would tell those people to walk a mile in my shoes. You try to deal with the soul-crushing boredom five nights a week, year after year, and get back to me. Especially when you're destined for greatness, but it seems the fates are out to get you.

Well, one fateful Friday night not too long ago, my time would finally come. I was working late, as usual. Filing, or cataloging, or making spreadsheets or some shit. I don't remember. I just remember my boss asking something of me, and then the familiar feeling of righteous indignation holding me in its grip like a fucking straight-jacket. Oh, how I hated him. And I hated my co-workers too. I thought they were all a bunch of do-nothing, go-nowhere bumps on a log. Like the human equivalent of oatmeal. I knew I was different than them, which is why I never made small talk. I just clocked in, put myself on auto-pilot, and clocked out. I put in my time, did the bare minimum, and counted the hours until I was free.

Let me tell you, nothing felt better than those night drives, especially the ones on Friday! To know I had two whole days to myself. Two days to do all the things in life that were far more important than wasting my valuable time on anyone at that idiot factory, casting my pearls to those swine. But I hadn't exactly been using my weekends to their fullest potential. I'd bought some new video games, and the past few weekends, I'd spent the entire time holed up in one room in my house, trying to beat them. I even beat one in a single sitting once! Don't get me wrong. It was fun. But it was a little disappointing when I realized, after beating it, that I had to be back at work in less than 12 hours.

It was then that I had the thought that all the time I'd spent indoors on the weekends had been doing something to me. Something good. All the time I had to sit and think about things made me feel like I'd cracked a code of some sort – a code that nobody else could see. And because of that, people were starting to annoy me. It seemed the whole world was populated by fools. Honestly, it swear that everyone I ran into was either an idiot or an asshole or both. I wondered if it was just me at first. But everywhere I went – every time I left the house – I'd run into another moron that was just taking up too space on the road, releasing toxic gas into the air with their banal small-talk, or not getting my food order right. The world was dying, and I seemed to be the only one paying attention.

One fateful Friday night, while driving home, I was deep in thought on the subject, wondering what exactly was wrong with everyone, and how I could fix it. And if I couldn't fixit, how could I ensure that I never had to deal with these people anymore? Surely there was a better way to live. Surely there were people doing it right. Living the kind of life that was bigger, and better, and truer. Living the kind of life where they never had to do anything they didn't want to do ever again. I mean, for fuck's sake, think about the act of taking out your trash! Is there anything more depressing than carting your own waste to the curb on a weekly basis? I couldn't wait for the day I'd have someone to do it for me.

All of these thoughts and more raced through my mind as I sat idling at a red light only a few blocks from my home. I had a game console with my name on it, and forty-eight hours all to myself to plot and plan for the impending greatness that I knew was my birthright. That's when I saw the blinking sign in the corner of my eye. Without thinking, I turned to look and it was only then that I was pulled from my thoughts.

To my left was a strip mall I'd passed a thousand times before. It was an L-shaped corner lot. Behind the lot was a block of homes separated by a large stone wall. It's one of those places you see almost every day, but have never stopped there to shop for anything. As I said, there was a blinking light. And I don't know if it was ever there before, or if it was newly installed, but that night I saw it. Fastened to the back edge of the building closest to me was a metal sign in the shape of a star, with bright bulbs outlining its perimeter. Beneath the blazing star was an arrow that pointed toward the alley behind the strip mall. Much like the sign itself, I never noticed the alley before. And as I sat staring, I saw in my periphery that the traffic light changed to green. I stayed focused on the sign. The name of the bar – THE CONSTELLATION – was blinking inside that star, practically shouting at me to heed its call. Heed I did.

I still don't know why. I couldn't say what propelled me there that night. The sign. The name.

The feeling of finding something new and exotic in a familiar environment. Or perhaps it's just shitty storytelling and my mind is frantically trying to fill in a gap in logic to protect me from the harsh reality of the padded cell I'm currently sitting in. All I can tell you is that it all felt right, somehow, for some reason. I parked in the shopping center, because as far as I could tell, the bare didn't have a lot of its own, and when I got out of my car, the first thing I noticed was that the air felt significant, yet fabricated. Crisp and clear, but somehow untrue. There wasn't a car in sight, in either direction. I couldn't even hear any traffic in the distance. Nor were there any nocturnal animals singing their midnight songs. It was almost like I'd stumbled onto the backlot of a movie studio that was a perfect replica of my neighborhood. It was eerie. I shook the feeling off, and went inside. I was never the same again.

The place was dark. I instantly loved the atmosphere. The interior was almost smokey, with some astoundingly warped acid jazz playing somewhere in the background. This was the kind of place that you would imagine was invitation only. I knew I was in my element from the get go. Everything was dark red leather, with deep rich wood wherever you looked. The place was small, but it packed a punch. Booths lined the back wall and ran the length of the room. There was only enough space left for a single pool table, upholstered in black cloth, which sat unused, between the bar and the booths. The bar itself was seemingly fashioned out of a grand knotty tree trunk, probably 30 feet in length. Wherever it had stood in its previous life, it couldn't have held a candle to the sight of where it sat now.

This was the place I'd been looking for my whole life. And it was right in my backyard! I knew immediately I would be spending a lot of time here in the future. I sidled on up to the bar, took a seat, and made myself comfortable. I was still looking around at the place, in complete awe, when the bartender's voice stirred me from my reverie.

"What can I get you," said the voice at my back.

I swung around on my stool and opened my mouth to place my order when I locked eyes with the bartender and realized I'd forgotten how to talk. The thing that stared back at me was not a man. Hell, it wasn't even man-like. It was a mountain of hair, with seven heads perched atop shoulders two door-frames wide. The heads were stacked like a row of skyscrapers, the tallest in the middle, with three heads tapering down either side to the left and right. Every head had only one eye, and when it spoke, each mouth uttered one of the words, seemingly at random.

"I

Said

What

Can

I

Get

You?"

What could I do? Would would *you* do? I just stared at the fucking thing. I'm pretty sure I didn't blink for a full minute. Maybe those seven heads are looking at someone else, I thought. Maybe he doesn't even see me! It's possible that I, a single headed organism, don't even register in his field of vision. But I looked at each of those seven heads, and one by one I saw an eye staring right back at me. Seven eyes. All focused directly on me. All wanting to know what I wanted to drink.

That was about the time I thought I felt a lot *more*

eyes on me. And that's when I took a real good look around, careful to focus on the rest of the clientele. I don't know how I hadn't spotted it before, but I guess I had only given a cursory glance to the customers. I was too wrapped up in savoring the experience. Plus I'm not big on eye contact, so I kept my head down when I enter places for the most part. But I looked at the room with fresh eyes, and I'm happy to report that I didn't see any more seven headed creatures. Though it was of little comfort, because there was a gill-man playing pool with an amorphous blob of dark matter in the middle of the room. And In the back booth, I could see a pair of 10 point horns cresting the top of a high backed chair. And from the shadows under that table I could make out the shape of cloven hooves. In the other booths I saw patches of scaly skin, something that was either a single creature with 12 legs, or 4 creatures with 3 legs. I still don't know the answer to that one.

But I think you get the idea. The whole place was crawling with monsters. And in some cases, monsters were literally crawling around the place. Much as I wanted to in that moment, I realized I couldn't leave my post and run screaming for the door. I was worried that would draw some unwanted attention. It made sense at the time, if the word is still applicable in any way, but I reasoned that if I just pretended that I didn't think anything was out of the ordinary, the rest of the patrons would feel the same, and then they wouldn't eat me or tear me limb from limb, or whatever monsters did for fun.

I resolved then to sit still and push my fear deep, deep down long enough to have a single drink. I would tip well. And then I would leave, and never tell another living soul just how insane I'd gone in the span of a single car ride home. So I turned back to the bartender, opened my mouth, and again found myself speechless. What the fuck recdo monsters drink? I couldn't very well order a hefeweizen. For some reason that felt tantamount to ordering caviar at a fried chicken restaurant. Very quickly I accessed all the fantasy films I'd ever seen in the hopes of naming something that sounded monstrous. Hell, if I ran into a vampire, you bet your ass I'd try the garlic and silver bullets. These things stick to the collective consciousness for a reason, right? Bearing that in mind, a few images popped into my rapidly deteriorating mind, and I finally looked the bartender in as many of his eyes as I could without maintaining uncomfortably long eye contact and said, " One mead please."

As soon as the words left my mouth I felt like the world's biggest asshole. This wasn't the fucking renaissance fair. What was I thinking? But without skipping a beat, the bartender set a large metal stein in front of me, uncorked a sizable clear glass jug, and poured a thick amber liquid into the stein. It looked like pure maple syrup and I could smell it from where I sat. It was cloyingly sweet, and the aroma actually made my mouth water.

As soon as the smell hit me, I began to panic all over again. How the fuck was I going to pay for the thing? I didn't know if this place took credit card or gold bullion, and I didn't want to ask, because I'd left all my bullion at home.

Fortunately for me, my panic was quickly overtaken by an even more intense kind of panic, when two of this fine establishment's patrons sat down on either side of me and one of them – one with an insanely deep voice - told the bartender that this one was on them. Sure, I was grateful that I didn't have to embarrass myself, or worse yet, admit that I might not be able to pay for my libation after all. But now I knew that I had been spotted, and worse yet, flanked. On the stool to my right, a satyr rested his elbows on the bar, placing his forelegs atop the stool. His hindquarters stayed planted on the ground.

To my left was a fully mobile robot that looked like a steel plated human skeleton. I could hear the distinct sound of soft bubbles coming from the brain floating in green liquid encased in glass atop his head.

Resigned to the fact that the robot was probably going to tear my limbs from my body and feed them to his friend the Satyr, as calmly as I could, I spoke.

"Thank you," I said, avoiding eye contact and taking a sip from my stein.

"The pleasure is all ours," said the robot in a male voice that had a comically effeminate Southern accent.

The mead hit my lips and it stung like fire. I coughed, though I'm still not sure if it was from the drink, the robot's statement, or the fact that, of these two nightmarish visions at my sides, I would have bet my life savings that the robot was the one with the deep voice.

"Easy," said the satyr.

All I could do was nod, putting the back of my hand to my mouth as my eyes watered. There it was. The voice the sounded like a bag of gravel being run through a clothes dryer. In my periphery, I could see that the Satyr had a thick black beard that ran all the way down to his chest. Maybe *he* would be the one to rip me apart and then he would feed me to the robot to keep its brain juices fresh. The robot spoke again.

"I'd wager you're new here.""

"Was it that obvious?" I asked. Feeing all the blood rush to my face.

"It is. But that's not a bad thing. I find it's the new ones that have the most fascinating stories."

"I find that hard to believe," I said, wondering where the words had come from and why I'd said them.

The Satyr laughed, though I wasn't sure it was from anything I'd said. He seemed to be in his own world.

"And why's that?" Asked the Robot.

"Oh," I said, before I could stop myself, "This place seems pretty fascinating itself. I don't know that someone like me would bring anything to the table."

"That's rich!" The Robot said stretching the two words out. "The grass really is always greener, isn't it?"

"Sometimes it really is," I said, defensively, wondering who the fuck had just hijacked my mind and body. Why was I talking? I should have just nodded and sipped my stein of magma flavored molasses. But something was brewing inside me. Even though every flake of my flesh quaked in terror at the position in which I'd found myself, I couldn't help but feel exhilarated at the same time. Whatever was happening, it was pretty fucking cool. Unless it was a total schizophrenic break. And the jury's still out on that one.

"If someone's grass is greener than mine, I just shit on it," Satyr said.

"Oh," I said. "I…uh-"

"Don't mind him," Robot said. "That's his answer for everything. He's always looking for an excuse to shit on something."

"That's not true," Satyr said.

"You shit on the troll in the riverbed on the way here!"

"He was a fucking asshole."

"Well I cannot engage in a battle of wits with someone who is unarmed, can I?"

"What?"

"Never mind. We're being rude and ignoring our visitor."

"Oh that's fine," I said. "Don't let me get in the way!" I was happy they'd forgotten about me for a moment. I'd even hoped it would last longer. Mostly because the conversation was so ludicrous. Nobody was going to believe any of this. I couldn't even believe it and it was happening to me.

"Nonsense!" Robot replied. "My friend here has lost the metaphor, but I remain curious: what's the grass we're discussing presently?"

"Grass? Oh. Right. I think I mean this place. That's number one, obviously."

"Why's that?" Robot inquired.

I took a second to respond. I knew if I answered, I would be crossing a border from which I'd never be able to return. I looked at the divide it in my mind, paused for a moment, and then took the leap. "Well, because all my life I suspected there were greater things. And now here I am. I lived for decades knowing that there was something out there for me. Something that the rest of the world was content not to concern itself with. But something that I wanted. I'm sick of seeing other people live lives they don't deserve, while I wait for my turn. And I think this place is the first step. At least, I hope it is."

"That's deep," Satyr said.

I laughed to myself. Robot spoke.

"I have to agree. I find that very profound. What's the second thing?"

"Second thing?" I asked.

"Reasons why you know the grass is greener. You said this place is number one. What's number two?"

"Ah. Yeah. Good question. I guess it's just the obvious stuff. You know? Some people have bigger houses. Some people get to take more vacations. Some people don't have to eat shit and pretend they like it."

"They do if they piss me off," Satyr said.

"I gathered that," I said, a smile on my lips.

"See what I mean?" Robot said. "But I digress. Everything is relative, is it not? Someone might have a bigger house, but that just means they have a bigger house payment. And maybe they're miserable. And all that means is they'd just have more rooms to cry in at night."

"Well sure," I said. "We can play that game all night long. It's nice to hope that the great wheel of Karma balances everything out, and even the fortunate have their struggles. But it doesn't change the fact that I deserve more!"

"Now we're getting to the meat," Robot said.

"Meat?" Satyr asked, his eyebrows perking up.

"No, Mortimer. It's an expression."

This time it was my eyebrows that perked up. This hulking, shitting beast was named Mortimer? This got better and better. I was already in for a penny, I figured I'd throw the whole pound in there.

"Oh, by the way, my name's Al," I said. "Pleased to meet you both."

"I'm Mortimer," Satyr said.

"And my serial number isn't very easy for folks to memorize," the Robot said, "So you can just call me Cy. As I was saying, I think we've touched upon something crucial here. You said you deserve more. By that regard, you're communicating that there is something you *don't* deserve."

"Shit," I said. "Now *that's* deep. I never thought about it that way. First thing that comes to mind is my job. Don't get me wrong. It pays the bills. But it's so god damn boring. And my boss does fuck-all, while he piles more work onto everyone else. We work our asses off, and he just gets fatter and richer."

"I see," the Robot said. "Al, how would you like to accompany Mortimer and me on an errand we must run this evening?"

And that was it. I was in. This was the invitation I'd been waiting for.

"Hell yes," I said, throwing back the rest of my mead. It hurt like a sonofabitch, but I was too excited to let that bother me.

We left the bar. I never did see what Cy and Mortimer paid with, but I like to imagine it was some form of lumpy, weathered precious metal. As we stepped back into the night air, it seemed I was looking at the world through new eyes. I felt I had sloughed off an old skin, and had stepped into a new form. One with a new purpose. It felt great.

"Where are you parked?" Cy asked.

"Just around the corner," I said. "Why?"

"Let's take your car," he said.

"Oh, Okay," I said, a little disappointed. I had pictured us traveling by flying car, or through the sewers on a boat made of whale bones or something. My car was decidedly less exotic. I led them to my little sedan, but when I got to my door, I realized that I was actually pretty well drunk.

"Um," I slurred.

"I will drive," Cy said, heading me off at the pass. He was very intuitive.

I pointed my finger at him and, half lidded, said, "You're alright, Cy!" Then I walked to the passenger side and hit the button on my fob to unlock the doors.

Cy got in, sat down, and put his seatbelt before I'd even opened my door. As I climbed in, Mortimer opened the door to the back seat. I didn't realize how large he was by comparison, and wondered how he was going to fit. But he answered the question for me when he tore out the entire back seat in one gesture and threw it onto the black asphalt of the parking lot.

My mouth formed the 'w' in "What the Fuck" but the words never left my lips because I remembered what he said about people who piss him off. I preferred to end my night not covered in satyr shit, so I shut my mouth and resigned to the fact that this was the price of greatness.

Mortimer climbed into the back of my now very spacious car and folded his four legs onto the exposed metal beneath him. I exhaled slowly, partially to stabilize myself from the effects of the firewater, and partially to mourn my car. But I climbed in, shut my door, and offered Cy my keys. That's when I saw him tear the paneling off my ignition, exposing the wiring beneath. He grabbed the wires and a jolt of electricity passed through his fingers, starting the car. Okay, so they weren't the kind of folks who were good with other people's things. That was fine. I didn't imagine they'd want to borrow any of my clothes, so it didn't matter. I resolved to let it go and stay focused on the bigger picture.

Cy put the car in drive, and we were on our way.

"Where are we going?" I asked, hoping the tone in my voice didn't sound like me making sure I didn't just sign up for my own murder.

"Business," said Mortimer, as if that answered my question.

"Mortimer speaks the truth, albeit succinctly. We have a date with an individual who owes us something."

As we drove to our destination, Mortimer and Cy instructed me on the proper etiquette for what was about to take place.

No crying.

No flinching.

And above all else, no talking.

It seemed they were going to bill me as their silent, and therefore toughest partner. I was terrified. I was positive this was a bad idea. As they explained everything to me, all I could do was stare and marvel at these bizarre creatures. Mortimer was a piece of work. He was obviously the brawn of the operation. The longer I looked at him, the dumber it seemed he became. Stealing glances at him in my rear view mirror, I noticed that he had a massive underbite that made his resting face look positively braindead.

Cy was a different story altogether. He was by his very nature, entirely inscrutable. What was he thinking? What was he feeling? *Was* he thinking or feeling? That great bubbling brain of his looked human, but it could have just as easily come from something like Mortimer, or one of the seven heads possessed by our bartender. Every second I was in this world gave birth to a dozen more questions. I couldn't recall a time where my imagination and curiosity were so alive.

While I was busy fixating on my traveling companions, the car came to a stop. I looked around and saw that we were in one of countless blocks of homes not far from where I lived. I'd probably driven through this street to avoid a traffic signal once or twice without thinking anything of it. It was as unassuming as could be, so I therefore found it a surprising destination.

"You sure you're at the right place?" I asked.

"One hundred percent," Cy said.

"Yuh," Mortimer agreed.

I couldn't argue with that. We all got out. Mortimer was as gentle exciting my car as he was getting in. Which is to say he muscled his way out of the back seat, tearing the cloth all along the back rest, and scratching the shit out of the floor beneath his feet. The car was already a lost cause, so I just continued to ignore it.

Cy led us up the driveway of the home we'd parked directly in front of. It was a plain Jane one-story house, which only gave birth to a dozen more questions. Was the person behind its door human? What kind of transaction was about to take place? And how had any business found its way to this house in the first place?

Cy knocked on the white wooden windowless door and after a few seconds a porch light came on and I could hear the sounds of locks being turned. The door opened a crack, and a single eyeball crept around the door and peered at us. That eyeball was attached to a long stalk that continued to reveal itself, until finally the head it was attached to could be seen.

"About fucking time," Eyeball said, in a nasally tone. "Was wondering if you guys would ever show up."

"When have we ever not shown up?" Cy said. "Now are you going to invite us in, or would you prefer to complete this transaction in the open?"

Eyeball swung his door open and that's when I got a good look at him. He looked like a four foot tall green beetle. He had two arms and two legs, each of which ended in serrated claws. His round head sat atop his body like a snowman's and at the top of his head, the long stalk that ended in a single eyeball danced around as he spoke through a mouth that opened sideways. I couldn't see anything beyond the threshold of Eyeball's. But Cy ushered me in first. No flinching, he'd said. So I pressed on.

The darkness was due only to a small room adjoining the entrance to the house. It was carpeted, and the ceiling was low and it felt more like an enclosed porch than anything else. When I walked through the second door – this one finally leading inside the actual home – I was horrified. The inside of the house was bland beyond belief. Other than that, there was nothing at all in this place to provide any evidence that a monster dwelled under its roof. The interior design was monstrous, I'll grant that. White carpet with black, plastic furniture. No art on the bare white walls. It was the ultimate bachelor pad. And by that, I mean it desperately needed a feminine touch. Though I didn't say any of this to anyone. I continued to keep my mouth shut, as instructed.

"Who's the square?" Eyeball said, his stalk rotating clockwise as he stared at me.

I steeled myself.

"He is our new supplier," Cy said. " You're going to enjoy this batch. It is some of the purest product I've ever seen."

Eyeball's stalk froze where it was and began to water, almost as though his very eye was salivating. He only hesitated a moment before tearing away to the black table in the middle of the room. He pushed aside a stack of books and lifted a panel, revealing a safe hidden in the table. As he worked the combination, the unmistakable scent of baby oil hit me. I ignored it. There were a lot of implications in that smell, and none of them were things I wanted to think about, so I pulled myself up out of the undertow of my thoughts, and focused again on the present. Eyeball was speaking.

"Y'know, I don't normally do this. But it's been a hard month, and I wanted to treat myself. Do you guys wanna join me?"

"I'm entirely incapable," Cy said.

"No," Mortimer grunted, and cracked his knuckles.

Eyeball shot a glance in my direction. I looked to Cy and Mortimer. We had gone off script. I didn't know what to say. I judged the situation as best I could and said, "I don't get high on my own supply," hoping that not only was it appropriate for the circumstances, but also that it didn't sound completely idiotic.

Eyeball looked at me, blinked once, and said, "Fine. No skin off my sacks. More for me."

And so saying, he opened the door to the safe, plunged his claws inside, and pulled out the two largest stacks of cash I have ever seen in real life, if that's indeed what this was. These stacks were each as long as a loaf of bread, rubber banded together. And from the looks of it, they were comprised solely of hundreds. I went rigid at the sight. I think I even forgot how to swallow for a moment. Eyeball handed the stacks to Cy who flipped through them in a heartbeat, like the world's most efficient counting machine.

"It's all there," he said, then handed the stacks to Mortimer, who gripped them both in one hand. Mortimer slid his free hand into his own skin and pulled a swathe of flesh away from the area beneath his belly button, revealing a marsupial-like pouch. He dropped the money into the pouch, then fished around for a short time, finally bringing up a velvety satchel about the size of an apple.

Cy took the pouch and handed it to Eyeball, who was working himself up now, but trying to keep calm. The sight made me feel zen by comparison. This guy had probably done this a few times in his life, but this was my first rodeo, and I was doing a better job of maintaining my composure than he was. But I think that's just what it looks like when you're jonesing. And this guy had it bad. Suddenly his story about the hard month had the distinct air of bullshit.

Cy extended his glimmering arm, and Eyeball snatched the bag with obvious lust.

"You sure you guys don't want in on this action?"

"Positive," Cy said.

Mortimer said nothing this time. I followed his lead.

"Guess I'm the only one that likes to have fun," Eyeball said, with a desperate laugh.

In one movement, he closed the safe door, opened the bag, and emptied its contents onto the coffee table. What came spilling out was a pile of the clearest, brightest diamonds I'd ever seen.

"Oh fuck, these are good!" Eyeball exclaimed. "Look at the fucking clarity on these!"

Then he picked up a clawful of the diamonds and squeezed them. I can still hear the sound of the diamonds as they popped and snapped in his grip. It hurts just to think about. He pulverized them into dust. I was shocked. I wanted to slap the diamonds out of his claw. I didn't understand what was happening until he looked back toward us with a gleam in his eye and a smile on his thin lips as he dipped the tip of his other claw into the power, brought the glimmering tip to his nose, and snorted it.

I have since read more about diamonds and their makeup and I couldn't tell you what possible side effect inhaling their dust might have on a body, but I don't know what Eyeball was made of. All I do know is that when that powder hit his nostrils, his single pupil exploded to black, fully dilating in an instant.

"You guys are so fucking lucky to know me," was the first thing he said after his bump.

That's when the baby oil smell came back. Cy and

Mortimer were fantastic beasts, to be sure, but their choice in company left something to be desired. Though I did take into account the fact that this was their job. Hell, like I said at the start, everybody hates their job, right? Maybe they were as put off by this ugly creature as I was, and they were counting the minutes until this gig was over.

As luck would have it, the those minutes were up.

"Indeed," Cy said. "Robert, it's always a pleasure doing business with you. Shall we book you for the same time next month?"

"What?" The one-eyed creature that was apparently named Robert said. "No. This ain't a regular thing with us. I told you. It was a hard month. I'll call you when I need you. If I need you. You can go now," he said, waving a claw at us, as he flitted around the house, pulling books from his shelves and collecting them in his claws. At the rate Bob was moving, he was going to read all of the books he'd pulled off the shelf in about fifteen minutes. And there were a lot of books. What he did after that was anybody's guess. Maybe he scratched his carapace to pictures of beetles fucking. I was just happy we were leaving.

"Of course," Cy said. "Enjoy. I imagine it will be a while before we see a batch this pure again. But you needn't worry about that. Hope to hear from you soon, old friend."

One-eyed Bob waved us out with the flick of a claw, muttering something to himself that sounded like the beginning of a conspiracy theory. I was the first one to the door, and I flung it open with a profound glee in my heart, hoping I would never cross paths with Beetle Bobby again.

As we crossed the threshold and walked down the

driveway back to my car, Mortimer spoke. "What was that line you said?"

I slowed my step, allowing Cy and Mortimer to catch up. I saw that Mortimer had his hands in his pouch and he was, I think, counting the money. But it looked more like a guy playing with his dick and balls under a blanket. It had a disquieting effect. I had no knowledge of proper centaur etiquette, so I didn't Share my thoughts. But I couldn't shake them either.

"Uh," I said, trying to remember the question. "Don't get high on your own supply?"

Mortimer laughed.

"It rhymes," he said.

It sure did.

"Lovely person, Robert," Cy said. His robotic tone was straight down the middle and I had no idea if he was being sarcastic, but I hoped to God he was.

"That was definitely interesting," I said. "How common is that? I've never seen anyone-"

"Everyone has device," Cy said. "Get it? Just a little joke to lighten the mood. I always need a palate cleanser whenever I visit Robert. And I guarantee you we will be right here, in this exact spot, one month from now."

A great relief came over me. I was happy to know I wasn't the only one that was skeeved out Bob.

"We have a lot of clients," Cy said. "And we specialize in hard to find items. It draws out the weirdos. But if they don't pay, or they get out of line-"

"Let me guess," I said. "Mortimer shits on them?"

"After," Mortimer said, without a trace of humor.

"After what?" I said.

"Better not to ask," Cy broke in.

All the questions I had dried up like a reservoir in a drought. As we approached the car, I realized my body felt tired. I think I'd been riding an adrenaline high for the past few hours, and I was close to crashing. I assumed we were done with our time together, but Cy, walking back to the driver's side of the car, looked to me and said, "I have a wacky idea."

I though we'd already done wacky. My curiosity was piqued.

"Yeah?" I said.

"Would you want to do this with us full time? It's always good to have an extra pair of eyes."

My heart surged. The universe had listened. I wasn't going to be like the chumps who missed their golden opportunities and lived mediocre lives. I seized my moment.

"Fuck. Yes." I said.

"Excellent," he replied. "Do you know where your boss lives?"

I narrowed my eyes, thinking. "Actually, yeah. He made me drop off some shit for him in the middle of the night once. Why?"

"Perfect,' Cy said. "You navigate. I think we should tender your resignation immediately."

I must have smiled the entire length of the trip. It was a thirty-five minute drive and my mind raced with the possibilities of what would happen next. As the night wind whipped through my hair, we blasted the stereo at full volume, and I felt more alive than I can ever remember. I felt like I'd just won the lottery. I'd happened upon this place, these people, these incredible circumstances, and now I was even about to be validated. This was too good to be true.

When we pulled into the right neighborhood, Cy turned the music down and shut off the headlights. As we drew closer to the house, Cy turned off the engine and let the car cruise to the curb a few houses down. I mean, I understood that we needed to keep a low profile, but I didn't think all of that superspy shit was entirely necessary.

"I like this neighborhood," Cy said. "What about you, Mortimer?"

Mortimer grunted without looking up and said, "I've got a good one brewing."

I could feel the smile on my face widen. My boss – King Dumb Luck – was about to get a heaping dose of satyr shit. Oh this was going to be sweet.

We all got out of the car. I could hear Mortimer scraping up the inside something fierce as he exited, but we were already past the point of no return there. And the destination we were about to reach made it all okay anyway. I felt like a high school senior on prom night, about to toilet paper the principal's house.

Cy reached the door first. I assumed he'd hit the doorbell, but instead, he jammed his mechanical finger into the lock of the door like he'd done with my ignition, then he flicked his wrist, and the door swung open silently.

Yes, technically we'd just crossed from whimsical pranking into light breaking and entering, but you only live once, right? And I'm pretty sure most folks don't get to pull all-nighters with a satyr and a cyborg. And if they did, half of those folks probably imagined it anyway. Maybe I'm eve one of them! But I'm straying from the point. A warning light was going off somewhere in my head, but I was too excited to pay attention to it.

We entered the darkened house, and shut the door behind us. As we made our way through the house, looking for the master bedroom, I noticed that Cy and Mortimer were very light on their feet. Neither of them could have weighed less than three hundred pounds, but they practically glided through the house, towards the closed double doors of the master bedroom like ballet dancers.

"Is your boss single?" Cy asked.

I nodded my head yes.

"Good," Mortimer growled. "The less collateral damage, the better."

I opened my mouth to ask what he meant, but we'd already reached the bedroom door and I didn't want to make any noise. Cy turned the knob and just as I snapped my mouth shut, his head lit up like a Christmas tree, and a siren went off that could have woke the dead.

Cy's head was so bright that I could instantly see the room in its entirety. And as I watched my boss fly out of bed in a frightened stupor, the first thing I thought was that we'd triggered his alarm system.But then I realized that the sound wasn't coming from the house. It was coming from Cy, who now began to speak. As he talked, it was as if he were shouting through a bullhorn.

"Wake up, asshole! Your number is up!"

My boss was backing himself into a corner, looking very much like a caged animal, when he finally seemed to focus his eyes on us and his shocked terror was replaced by a distinct confusion.

"Al?" He said.

"Hey Keith," I replied, nonchalant. I would never have the upper hand like this again, and I wasn't about to waste it. I wondered if he would tell anyone what happened on Monday..

"What the fuck, Al? Is this supposed to be funny? I-"

Keith's words seemed to catch in his throat there, because that's when Mortimer walked in. I didn't realize he wasn't in the room yet, but I'm sure the sight of a nearly seven foot tall, four-legged man-beast was something that Keith would need some time to process. I knew that because I was still processing it, and I'd spent my entire night with him.

"Keith," I said pointing to my right, "Meet Mortimer." Then, gesturing to my left, "And Cy. They're my new friends."

"Hello Keith. I've heard so much about you," Cy said, as he took a step forward.

Keith loosed a shriek I didn't know a grown man was capable of. I don't think he realized the blinking pile of steel at my side was alive until that moment. It was hysterical. I swear he was going to piss himself.

"What is that?" He shouted.

"You're not listening," I said. "That's Cy. And be careful. You're liable to hurt his feelings."

"I regret to inform you that the damage has already been done," Cy said. "And Mortimer here has something he would like to say about that."

Mortimer grunted, then lumbered forward. "I've been baking this one all night," he said.

"Al, what's happening?" Keith said. "Is this some cosplay bullshit? Are you high or something?"

"Keith," I said, "Consider this my resignation. I'm on to bigger and better."

Mortimer continued his advance, and Keith continued his retreat. But very quickly he'd backed himself into the corner of his room. I couldn't wait to watch that giant satyr drop a steaming pile onto Keith's carpet. Which, in hindsight, I recognize is not a healthy thought.

"What the fuck?" he screamed again. "Al! Al! Al!"

"It's okay, Keith. Relax" I assured him. "It's not that bad. We'll be gone before you-"

But before I could finish my sentence, Mortimer grabbed Keith's head, and caved it in like an overripe pumpkin. Keith didn't even have a chance to protest.

The last thing he said was my name, and then a giant monster crushed his skull and his lifeless body dropped to the ground like a bag of old bed sheets. I couldn't speak. I couldn't think. All I could do was replay the image of Keith's terrified face as Mortimer's claw reached out for him. His eyes. The blood. The way his body hit the ground. It was all so terrible. I couldn't believe it.

It was a different kind of disbelief than when I'd walked into the bar at the start of the night. A different kind of disbelieve than seeing all these marvelous creatures. This was the kind of disbelief you feel when you're grieving. When something or someone is lost and will never return to you. I mourned for Keith. He was a dipshit, but he wasn't a bad guy. He didn't deserve this. I thought I was just going to flirt with disaster and, well, I don't know what else. I didn't think that far ahead. I was so certain of my call to greatness that I had blinded myself to the fact that I was in the company of genuine monsters.

I wanted out. I wanted to turn back the clock. I wanted my old, bland predictable life back. What the fuck was I doing here?

As Keith's body lay twitching and bleeding out on the floor, Mortimer swung his hind legs around, lifted his tail, and made good on his promise. He shit all over Keith's body. There was so much of it. And the smell – oh God, the smell. Satyr shit, and probably some of Keith's, and the blood. It was overpowering. I was going to puke.

I ran from the room, sealing my mouth shut with my hands, but the vomit came out anyway. My stomach lurched, and it shot up and sprayed out from between my fingers. As I knelt down at the wet patch on Keith's carpeted hallway floor, smelling my own sick combined with the shit and the blood, I realized something: I was right in the middle a crime scene. And I was leaving DNA everywhere. Fingerprints. Footprints. My own puke. How had I found myself in so fucking deep, so fucking fast?

This wasn't fun. This wasn't funny. This wasn't fantasy. This was fucking real life and it was too much for me to bear.

Cy and Mortimer were walking out of the room then, laughing to each other. I must have missed the joke. Or maybe I was the joke.

"What seems to be the problem?" Cy said, sounding earnest enough.

Mortimer said nothing. I looked up and saw that he was in his own world, making small, hideous grunts of pleasure as he licked the blood from his fingers. I thought I was going to vomit all over again.

"Shall we?" Cy said. "We have another appointment."

I knelt there, half hunched over, staring at the two of them. My whole body was shaking. I couldn't go with them. And I knew that when I told them as much, that would be it for me. But it was either face the music at that moment, or shortly after whenever I finally snapped. I chose to rip the bandage off.

"I...I can't," I finally said. "I thought this was something else."

"I see," Cy said, noticeably upset. "And what, exactly, did you think this was?"

"I don't know. Not this." It was all I could muster.

The two of them stood there, staring down at me. In the moonlight, half-lit, taking up the entire hallway, I fully understood for the first time in my life what the word 'monstrous' meant. These two were fucking terrifying. And I was in their sights. I suddenly felt like a child, seeing how close he could bring his finger to a campfire without getting burned. I was a fool. And pretty soon I'd be a dead fool.

"That's a shame," Cy said. "I was so looking forward to working together, Al. I feel you should know that we operate somewhat behind the law. If we part ways now, we can't guarantee that there won't be repercussions."

I sat there, on my knees, my mouth open. I could feel the chunks of puke stuck in my sinuses. I didn't understand why he wasn't moving in for the kill. Why neither of them were. But I didn't want to say anything that might change their minds, so I said nothing, only nodding stupidly.

"So be it," he continued. "I do hope our paths cross again some day. I like you, Al. Come on, Mortimer.."

Mortimer growled in accord and they started walking.

"Oh," Cy said as he passed me. "We'll be keeping the car."

I nodded again, mouth still open in astonishment. I was going to live. I don't know how, or why, but God damnit I was going to live!

When Mortimer passed me, he lifted his tail and ripped a fart so loud it blew my hair back and made my eyes water. The stench was ungodly.

Cy and Mortimer disappeared around the corner, and I stayed in that position until I heard my car start and drive off a few minutes later. Then I collected myself, wiped my prints from every surface I could remember touching, and crept out of the house. I walked home, sticking to the shadows all the way home. It took me hours to get there, but I was propelled by my confusion, and my fear. I didn't feel safe. I didn't know how anything would ever be right again. Mostly I stared into space, feeling like a man drowning. I also replayed the events of the night in my head over and over again. And when I wasn't doing either of those things, I was planning the rest of my life.

When I entered my home, the reality of it all finally sank in. Everything in my house was exactly as I'd left it, except for me. I didn't feel like I belonged there anymore.

I dropped to my knees and wept. It was as though I was trying to cry the ugly, unavoidable truth away. When I had completely emptied myself, I showered, climbed into bed, and watched the sun rise. My alarm went off. I showered again. And then I called the police and reported my car stolen. Then I waited for the cops to come.

Everything else played out like a dream. The cops came. I told them I woke up and the car was gone. They took my info and let me know that my car would likely never be recovered. They didn't know the half of it.

Then a second set of cops showed up. And they had questions. These were the cops I'd been waiting for. They told me some very unsettling news about my boss, Keith, and asked if I knew anything about it. I apologized for my behavior. I was recently the victim of a crime. But, my oh my, officer, this sure puts things into perspective. What kind of person could do such a thing? Life is so fragile, etc.

They thanked me for my time, and I have yet to hear from them, or Cy and Mortimer.

And here I am, sitting in my house on a Saturday night, sharing this story in between level-ups on the new RPG I just bought. I used to love first person shooters. Those are the video games play out from your POV while you navigate your way through an escalating body count. But they make me throw up now. I like the ones where you wander through a fantasy world collecting points and making virtual friends. It's the perfect metaphor for my life now. Actually, I'm not sure if that's even a metaphor.

I'm still waiting for the cops to come back. Or for Cy and Mortimer to come bursting through my door, Cy speaking in that disaffected, gentle southern accent as Mortimer, with a gut full of steaming shit, unloads onto my still-twitching corpse. I used to look everywhere and yearn for what others had. I was positive that everyone around me had it better, and that I deserved more. Now I know that I don't deserve shit. I'm lucky for every day. For every moment. I have everything I need. Hell, after Keith's body was discovered, upper management just shifted the staff one position upward. So I even got a promotion out of the whole hideous mess. I'm making more money, and the hours are better. And all I can do is wish it hadn't come at such a steep price.

I've never been back to The Constellation, either. Truth be told, I haven't even driven past it since that night. I take different paths to and from work. I shop at different stores. I do everything I can to avoid thinking about any of it. But it doesn't help. Whenever I'm at the office, or driving home, or sitting down on my couch firing up my console, I'm watching. I'm listening. I'm waiting for that knock on the door. Or that phone call.

Like I said, I appreciate everything I have. And all I want in the world is to be able to hang onto my tiny slice of gloriously simple living. I guess I'm just one of those people whose lessons need to come at a price. Though I do like to think that my suffering is enough to keep the scales balanced. There really isn't a day I wake up that I don't hear Keith's screams echoing in my head. And there isn't a paycheck I cash that doesn't remind me of the blood on my hands. Fuck extravagance. Fuck destiny. Let me live out the rest of my days having learned my lesson. And let my silent agony be enough.

Oh, and if I am indeed in a psych ward somewhere, this is most definitely a cry for help. I think my Thorazine dosage is too low. I can still smell the shit, Nurse. I can still hear the screams, Doctor.

I used to think I knew better than most people. I used to think I was too good for the world. Now? Now I just play my video games. I don't like to rock the boat. I've seen behind the curtain, and I all I want to do is live my quiet, simple life. Did I mention I even relish taking out my trash now? It reminds me of my place in the world. It's just so perfectly normal . . .

What The
Body Does

He sits in the crowded bar. He is surrounded by chatter. Everybody talks, but nobody says anything. They're all just people waiting for their turn to speak. He isn't here for them. He's here for her.

She sits across from him, a table between them, staring into his eyes as men who wear pants designed for women bump into him and spill their ironically cheap beers on his shoes. He stares back at her, ignoring the show put on around him. This is not his scene. And if all goes well, he'll never come here again.

As they talk, she crosses and uncrosses her legs. He can smell her from across the table. She's nervous. He likes that. It's so much better when they're nervous. The little ticks that come out - those unconscious social cues - are on full display. And they always think their poker face is an impenetrable force field that doesn't leak out in a thousand other areas.

But she's leaking.

He realizes he's been in his head too long. He redirects his attention, focusing his eyes on her mouth. She's spewing some bullshit about maturity. As if she has any idea.

"...I dunno, y'know?" she's saying. "I've just always felt like an old soul."

"Oh yeah," he replies, not missing a beat. His feigned enthusiasm would impress even the most seasoned actor. "I noticed that about you. I'm kind of an old soul myself."

"Totally," she says, leaning in. "I'm just tired of dating *boys*. I'm at a point in my life where I'm ready to take the next step. That probably scares the shit out of you, doesn't it?"

He smirks. There isn't much that scares him. He leans in. He takes her hand. With a smile on his thin lips, he says, "Let's get out of here."

She smiles back. He feels her body go rigid in a paroxysm of excitement; the inner tension of playing it cool. Then her face drops.

"I would. But I can't tonight. I need to-"

"You don't have to lie to me," he says.

She blushes and looks away as she protests, giving herself away completely, "What? Why would I-"

"I *know*," he says.

"You...know what?" she asks.

Sincerity is in her voice again. She really has no idea.

He doesn't move. He is the best salesman you've never seen. He is the god of Zen.

With a straight face and a voice like butter he quietly says, "I know that you're...you know. I can smell it from here."

Her eyes widen in shock. Before mortification can take over, he jumps back in, interrupting the thought. He is in control.

"It's not *you*. It's me. I'm...sensitive. Always have been. When I was a child another kid could skin his knee on the other end of the playground and I could smell it. But it's not a problem for me. In fact, it's what

you might call the opposite of a problem. It's sort of…
my thing."

She turns her head and looks slightly over her
shoulder in that gesture of recalibration suggesting
uncertainty, even if just for a moment. He spots it and
zeroes in. He's not about to let the line go slack on this
prize tuna.

"I know what you're thinking," he says. His
intensity has shifted gears. He's redirected it. He can't
want it too much. It's the wanting it that scares them
away. "Right now," he continues, "you're considering
everything society has forced upon you. That it's
disgusting and shameful and something you need to
hide away and keep a secret from men because it will
scare them off. But it's *all* conditioning. Otherwise
how will advertisers get us to be good little
consumers? Think about this: Since the day you were
born, you've been subject to commercials, and
magazine ads, and billboards that have molded you.
Now, I want you to forget all of that.

"Imagine that none of those things exist. Clean
slate. Now tell me how you actually feel, not just how
you've been told to feel." He sits back. He's done
everything he can do. He lets the silence between
them speak. He'll know if he's getting lucky tonight
in 5…4…3…2…

"Let's go," she says, wearing her newfound
defiance like a coat that's a few sizes too large.

———

When he opens the door to his place, they're already
kissing. He has one arm wrapped around her while
the other pushes open the door, granting them access
to the tiny studio apartment. Spartan is too opulent a
word for this place. The room contains a futon, a

mini-fridge, and four blank walls. She never notices. His strong arms are pulling her close to his taut, muscular body. He's firm with her, but gentle where he needs to be. Together, they move like an ocean, and she is swept away.

"My god, you're a good kisser," she says as she smiles and backs into the room.

"I'm good with my mouth," he says. "You'll see."

"You make that sound like a threat," she says, giving herself over to him more with every thrust.

At that, he kicks the door closed behind him and pushes her onto the futon. She lands on the padded covering, giggling with her legs in the air. She's wearing a skirt and he catches a flash of her panties before she loosely locks her knees together. They're black. Cotton. The color's right, but the cut does nothing for him.

"Don't' move," he says.

"What if I move a little bit?" she says, crossing her knees coyly, obstructing his view with a knowing smile.

"Then I'll have no choice but to beg you."

He gets on his hands and knees and crawls to her, his eyes never straying from the prize. He reaches her and kisses her feet. She laughs out loud. They always do. She presses the soles of her feet to his shoulders. This is where he gets excited. His heartbeat quickens. He tries to get closer, but she pushes back.

"Are you sure?" she says, biting her fingernail.

It's a gesture that could be misconstrued as playful to the untrained. But this is really the obligatory final check. Words won't do in a situation like this. They only cloud thoughts with projections and misinterpretation. Instead, he says nothing, and by way of reply he licks her ankle and runs his hand up her leg, sliding aside the panties and slipping a finger into her.

She moans and presses her inner thighs against his head.

She's wearing a pad, so the entry was easy. Every hygiene product has something for him to enjoy. Tampons require a bit more work, but they do collect every last drop in a tidy little carrying case like a box of fruit juice from concentrate. Pads are messier, which can be fun in their own right when he wants to drink straight from the tap. Sanitary cups are, of course, the greatest invention he's seen in his lifetime, but they are unfortunately rare.

In a single deft motion he pulls his finger out of her, taking her panties at the same time. He does this for a reason. He knows he should wait. He's only moments from reaching the Promised Land, but he can't help himself. Making sure that she doesn't see him, he runs his tongue along the side of his finger. A ripple of pleasure passes through his body. She's like a warm, young dessert wine.

Every woman is different, you see. They range from dryly sour to sickly sweet. He typically prefers a nice middle ground. Women are like days, and each one comes with its own set of singularities. Today, it just so happens, he's in the mood for sweet. And he could tell just by the smell of her that he would not be disappointed with her bouquet. He moves his head left, then right, kissing alternate thighs as he climbs ever closer to his bliss. She moans in acceptance. He's nearly home, but then he feels her knees lock together like a bear trap being set off. She's blocking his passage. He attempts to ignore what her body is telling him.

"Um," she says, "There's blood on your face."

Fuck. He knew it was a mistake to taste her so

early, but he couldn't help himself. The need made him do it. It's a part of him. It always has been. He doesn't know why he needs it. He only knows that it separates him from everyone else he's ever met.

"I'm just gonna go," she says, sitting up while pulling her skirt down.

His posture shifts in an instant. The cool customer has disappeared, replaced by someone else entirely. Now he's calculating. Remote. Hungry.

"I'm sorry," she says, starting to stand. "I thought I could-"

"It's fine," he says with a faux smirk. "Occupational hazard."

"I hope that's a joke," she says, standing up and pushing him away at the same time.

"Please don't," he says.

"No. I'm- this is done."

"I'm afraid I must insist," he says, his tone firmer.

She balks. "Insist?"

She shakes her head and makes a motion toward the door. Before she can take a step, he reaches out, places his hands on either side of her face, and twists, breaking her neck in an instant. Her eyes roll back inside her skull and her body drops to the futon like a pile of soiled linens.

He prefers to drink when they're still alive, but it's not a deal breaker. He spreads her legs, hitches her skirt up, and laps at her entrance. He's disappointed to find that there isn't much to be had. It means he'll be hungry again soon. But he puts the thought out of his head and sups, enjoying what he has while he has it.

———

He has a spot in the woods where he buries the ones he kills. He's had many spots over the years. It takes him a day to get there. He doesn't like the drives. There's too much time to think about the past, and all the questions he has that will never be answered about his existence. He was born of human parents, but they've been gone so long he's forgotten their faces. Humanity is a blur that continues to ebb and flow - to wither and die - around him. All the while his appetite lives on, and so does he: a monster adrift, never knowing where he came from, or where he's going – only that he is different.

And though he *is* different, he's not entirely inhuman. He feels loneliness, misery (and its counterpart, joy) and sometimes ponders the possibility of pairing with another and attempting a monogamous lifestyle, but his agelessness would make it difficult, and his thirst renders it an impossibility. And so the thought always passes like a kidney stone, causing its internal pain as it leaves him. He hopes it will never return again. But it always does, eventually.

By the time she's deep in the earth and he's close to home again, the questions and the thoughts have taken a back seat to the hunger that has gripped him once more. It came on suddenly and he isn't sure why. One meal, even a slight one, is usually enough to last him a few weeks. But it's not outside the realm of possibility that he'd need to feed again. The hunger must be heeded, and he's nothing if not resourceful. Instead of going home, he heads downtown. He passes the gentrified buildings covered in street art. He passes the skyscrapers that remind him of glass coffins. He finds his way into the heart of the city. And when he's in the area even *he* doesn't want to drive through, he knows he's in the right place. He slows his car to a crawl when he sees the first signs of buyable flesh.

The women on these corners and back alleys are repulsive to him. As a rule, he avoids paying for his meals, but he hopes that he'll find what he's looking for. As he cruises the streets, he passes bodies that reek of the wrong kinds of secretions. If he could, he'd find a stray dog and drain it of every ounce of blood, but that's not how his hunger works. He knows the stories about creatures of the night who feast on blood and are repelled by various Judeo-Christian icons, and whether those stories have any validity or are mythic distillations of his condition and needs, he has no idea.

What he does know is that he can't drink any old blood that crosses his path. It's not for want of trying, but there's something within the clotted, cyclical sanguinity alone that keeps him alive. He's thought about the metaphor of it all. The fact that it is a representation of new life, stripped away and sloughed off to give way to yet more life. Whatever science or magic lays behind his digestive system, he is only certain of one thing: It's imperative that he finds something to eat soon or he's liable to become sloppy. He can't have that. Loose ends are the wrong kind of bloody mess.

As he drives, the women call out to him. He ignores their sales pitches. Unless they're traveling with their monthly visitor, he wants nothing to do with them. The pickings are slim and he's already strategizing his next move. He might go to a mall. Maybe a nice, dark movie theater. There has to be a sporting event ending soon. The parking lots are always chaotic. People can get lost so easily. It's never an ideal plan of attack, but the snatch and grab is useful in times of need.

Right around the time he's trying to remember if there's a park nearby, an enchanting perfume breaks into his thoughts. He snaps his gaze in its direction and sees her standing alone at the end of the block. The body language says it all. She's got three items for sale in the whole store and one of them is busted. But you know what they say about trash and treasure.

He comes to a stop and looks at her like a man at a drive-thru ready to order from the secret menu. She approaches as he rolls down his window, her body language cool, but guarded.

"Hey," she says.

Her voice is a placatory lilt. She twists her body in a girlish affectation that says *I may look like a moth-eaten towel, but I'm really just a Lolita at heart.* The insincerity of it all almost ruins his appetite. But the appetite won't die that easily.

"Get in," he says.

She stays by his window in a half crouch and bunches her face into a sickly-sweet seduction. When she speaks again, that girlish lilt is in full effect.

"I only want you to put it in my ass. Can you do that for me? I love it when-"

"Drop it," he says. "Get in."

The waif disappears in an instant. In her place is a seasoned pro. She nods her head and drops the artifice.

"Ten for a handie. Twenty for a blowie. Fifty for the back. And I'm offering a discount on the front this week. That's thirty."

He's satisfied to have an honest reaction out of her. He pulls out his wallet and slides three ten-dollar-bills through the slit in his window. She grabs the bills, pockets them, steps off the curb, and walks around to the passenger door where she lets herself in.

"Go around the corner," she says. "There's an underground garage we have a deal with."

Silently he follows her instructions. He knows he shouldn't be this sloppy. He should have at least dropped the shovel off at his apartment. But The Need supersedes logic. The Appetite rules all.

He drives his car down into the dank garage. It's old, dark, and deserted. It's perfect.

"Take off your panties," he says.

"Um," she says.

She's looking for the right words, but words don't come easy to her. If they did, maybe she would have said *no* at some of the forks in the road of her life. He doesn't have time for her low-grade processor to string a few monosyllabic words together.

"I said," as he speaks, he reaches up under her form-fitting skirt, grabs the crotch of her panties and rips them down her legs.

"Hey!" she objects.

He does not relent.

They tear at the seam, coming free from her. He sees the pad. He sees the spotting. His breath catches in his throat, and he swears his heart stops beating in that split second between seeing the ambrosial red and pressing it to his face.

She tastes exactly as you might imagine. There is, of course, the copper tinge of blood. But there's also the sweat and filth from a long night of shopping her wares around town. The third taste is equal parts both and neither. It's powdery and it's sour and it's a flavor that a creature like her has no business owning.

He realizes he's making little grunts of contentment as he licks his plate clean.

With the wave of adrenaline now cresting, he suddenly remembers he's not alone. He looks to her and sees, to his surprise, she's not horrified. She's not even fazed.

"Don't let me interrupt," she says. "Whatever gets you off, daddy."

Her jaded reaction sparks a rage in him so sudden that it surprises even him. In a single fluid motion he reaches his hand up the back of her head and hammers her face down onto the dashboard. The blow knocks her unconscious. He throws her head back, spreads her legs, and consumes her. He can hear her rasping breaths as he drinks her down.

When he comes up for air, there's something wrong.

He's still not satisfied.

He doesn't understand what's happening. Two in a row is rare for him, and it's always been more than enough, regardless of density. And yet, right now, it isn't. Right now the dissatisfaction is maddening. He'd be worried if his mind weren't so clouded by frustration and starvation. It's as though both meals were so lacking in substance that they only served to make him hungrier. Angrier. He throws open the passenger door and pushes her out of the car. She lands on the humid asphalt floor. He pulls out of the garage, and drives away as cool and as quiet as his hunger will allow.

———

As he makes it back to his place, the coolness and the quietude have diminish by volume. The hunger is steadily demanding to be satisfied by any means necessary. He's fighting his biology and he's losing the battle. He also has a dirt-covered shovel in the trunk of his car and the DNA of a prostitute on his face, but the only thing on his mind is Plan C.

He pulls into the single-car garage of his apartment unit, grinding his passenger mirror into the wall. The mirror falls to the ground in a mess of broken glass. He makes a mental note to clean it up later.

Though his appetite has nothing to do with fetish, there is a place where people with a certain menstrual predilection can congregate in safety. While he is certain they don't share his particular set of needs (or even, perhaps, the same taxonomic rank), what they do have in common is that they only see life in shades of red. He signs in and starts fishing.

myscarletgospel: having a tough night. looking for a rose in bloom. anyone out there?

The_Ruby_Cardinal: PREACHING 2 THE CHOIR.

The_Ruby_Cardinal: ITS LIKE THEY ALL FUKN SYNCHED CYCLES AT THE SAME TIME.

AlwaysInHeat99: ...F4M here...In full bloom...Wanna cam?

myscarletgospel: looking for a more personal encounter, Always.

The_Ruby_Cardinal: GOOD LUCK, DUDE. ALWAYS, I'LL TAKE THAT ACTION. MESSAGING U NOW

The_Ruby_Cardinal has left the conversation.

AlwaysInHeat99 has left the conversation.

xxCrimsonDahliaxx: I'm glad they're gone. I prefer to be alone.

myscarletgospel: i see that you live nearby.

myscarletgospel: are you in need of a friend?

myscarletgospel: hello?

xxCrimsonDahliaxx: What's your address?

He hesitates for a moment. He's never given the address out online. The site is nowhere near secure. But she's the best option he's got right now. His stomach cramps up, taking a bite out of itself. He groans and gives her the address, his hand shaking as he punches the keys. It seems to take an eternity to get the information to her. But he does, and then he waits.

———

When she finally arrives he has worked himself into a frenzy. She rings the doorbell and he practically pulls the door off its hinges to let her in.

"Scarlet?" she asks with a shy smile.

She's enormous. He didn't expect anything different. Her appearance makes no difference to him. It's not about how the body looks. It's about what the body does. He extends his arm in a welcoming gesture.

"Dahlia," he says, a tremor barely audible in his once impenetrable delivery. "Please come in."

She nods, sucks in her lips and enters, avoiding eye contact. She hasn't done this very much. He can tell.

"I don't-"

"Do this often," he says, finishing her sentence. "I know. Neither do I," he lies. "Take off your panties."

"What?" she says, taking a step back from him.

Back in the parking garage, his hunger was enough that he'd run out of patience for pleasantries. That was a lifetime ago and he was feeling positively genteel in comparison to the need that's running through his veins now.

"I said. Take. Off. Your panties." His voice is severe.

She's not having fun. She stammers, "I...I..."

"It's a simple request," he says. With every step he takes toward her, she takes one back. "It's the social contract. We discussed an arrangement. I invited you over to my home. I don't need to know when you got off the bus or what your favorite type of wine is. I'll be able to glean that soon enough. Right now, I just need you to take your panties off and give me the blood."

Her face falls. She looks him in the eyes. He can see it in her expression before she even says it, and cold chills run down his body. That's when he realizes he can't smell her. He was too hungry to even think about its absence. His body goes rigid with rage.

"You're not-"

"I didn't think you meant *that*," she says.

His hands clench into fists at his sides.

"You said you were lonely," she goes on. " I thought you were just like me. I'm lonely too. And we can have fun together. I'll do whatever you want..."

She is the most pitiful creature he's ever seen. But any empathy he might have had the capacity to feel for her has burned away in a red-hot rage. He stands there starving while she gluts herself on his time. He realizes she's still talking.

"...I can go to the store and get some red dye and a funnel. I've read about Uncle Flo. I'd be happy to do that for you if that's your thing. Please. Just let me try and make you hap-"

He doesn't even feel himself choking her. He sees it happening as though he's watching a movie, or viewing some twisted version of himself in a dream. He hears the distant sounds of bones breaking and flesh squelching, but the hands responsible for this act are so far away from where his mind has retreated that they couldn't possibly belong to him. He isn't remorseful. He isn't alarmed. He's just hungry, and afraid of what will happen to him if he doesn't eat.

Her body hits the floor so hard that he'd be grateful he lived on the first floor if he had any rationale left in him. He leaves her there on the ground as he exits his apartment and. His door is open for all the world to see his indiscretions. He doesn't care. He's already walking toward the nearest street corner.

He has a new plan. It's the only plan that matters. He will find the first female creature he can and devour it whole, regardless of species or location. He'd go down on a panda bear in Times Square right now given the chance.

His directive is interrupted in an instant when a powerful smell washes over him. It makes his knees buckle. The smell is upon him before he even sees its source. But he knows she's there. He's never smelled anything like it in his long, secret life. It's honeyed and metallic and warm and it smells like life, death, and rebirth all rolled into one apocalyptic gale force wind that first knocks him backwards and then gently catches him in its arms right before he hits the ground.

Underneath all of that, everything in his being is telling him to run.

Every self-programed interior alarm system that he's learned to avoid detection in this life is screaming at him full volume.

Go.

Now.

This smell is your end.

These voices, however, do nothing to aid the hunger, which is so powerful now that he's beyond hope. The instant the miasma hit him his fate was sealed. He knows it. And he doesn't care. If this is the scent of oblivion, her taste is surely a revelation, and her embrace need not be feared. That's when he sees her, almost as though his thoughts were a summons.

She stands - a vision in the warm night air -

silhouetted by the moon at her back. Her features are angular and her movements sharp, birdlike. She wears a white, sleeveless sheath dress as though she were a harbinger, come from some unknowable future to deliver a life-altering message. For all he knows, she is. As she stands there, the skirt of her dress billows in the wind and he realizes then that she's a fine approximation of a woman. She'd fool any living man, but like knows like, and he sees in an instant the little details that create the preternatural perfection that's all too telling. She's far from human, though what she is, he could not say. He's never met another like himself. And now he's certain he never will.

Like a moth to the flame, he goes to her. Silently, she takes his hand in hers. He wants to say something, but his hunger controls him now, and his hunger has nothing to say except that one prevailing directive: feed me.

Stepping out in front of him, she guides him back toward his apartment. He staggers behind her, entranced. There is nothing else in the world except the two of them and this moment. She ushers him back inside his tiny dwelling and, as he steps over the threshold, she closes the door behind her and snaps the deadbolt shut. In a single graceful motion she turns to him and flicks the spaghetti straps of her dress off both shoulders. The garment falls like a curtain revealing her flawless nude body.

Her eyes lock with his as she reaches two fingers down between her thighs and touches her sex. The body of the Crimson Dahlia lays in a heap not two steps behind him, but his encounter with her was a lifetime ago. He watches, transfixed, as the Perfect Creature lifts her hand and shows him the glistening red moisture on her fingers. Her cup overflows.

He rushes her, desperate to put the fingers in her

mouth. He grabs her wrist. She grabs his in turn and, with physical strength matching the strength of her odor, she easily overpowers him. He's surprised to find that he doesn't care. An affront like this would have sparked a violent outburst in him only minutes ago. But here, with her, he is happy in his newfound weakness. He has surrendered.

She undresses him, pulling off each article of clothing slowly, teasingly, until his frenzy is beyond compare. Soon he is nude, standing and erect. Using his clothes, the preternatural woman binds his feet together, and then ties his hands behind his back. At last, she makes him lie down.

He obliges, happy to fulfill any request she might make of him. He lies on his back, nudging the Dahlia out of his way in the process. With his last unused article of clothing, the preternatural woman binds the cloth manacles of his hands to that of his feet, completely restricting his range of motion. He cannot move, and he does not care. His only concern is the unspoken promise of her scent; the message written in the glistening moisture on her fingers. His last supper.

He's never been harder than when she positions herself over him, and squats down, presenting to him the greatest view in all of creation. The smell hits him like an atom bomb. The storm wind that first bowled him over is pitiful by comparison to the tsunami that has overcome him. He strains to reach her. He tries like mad to pull his hands free.

To sit up.

To get just an inch closer to that paradisiacal chasm.

Then he sees it; a single drop of thick purplish blood collecting at her opening. He watches, paralyzed with lust and hunger as it grows, beads, and at long last frees itself from her. He watches, too, as it falls, his mouth open in greedy anticipation. The droplet lands on his tongue and his eyes roll into the back of his skull in the only moment of true bliss he has ever known. He has never touched a drug in his long, dark life, but he imagines this is the high that a junkie would spend his life chasing. The drop seems to coat his tongue, travel down his throat, and sink deep, past flesh, past bone, directly into his marrow. He wants with all his being to make this moment last for all time. It's a yearning so deep that he understands what it must be like to love and to lose love.

His hunger is satiated in an instant.

The satisfaction is fleeting.

As quickly as his eyes rolled fluttering to the back of his skull, they snap back to the fore, pupils fully dilated.

The drop is like a hit of napalm.

At first, the taste was everything he knew it could be, suddenly it is too much and he wants it gone. He tries to spit it out. He tries to scrape it off his tongue with his teeth. But no matter what he does, the heat spreads, covering his tongue, and traveling down his throat.

He looks up at his death and tries to ask her what she is and who sent her. As if in reply, she sprays a torrent of thick, black blood that hits him like a hose turned on high.

And in a heartbeat, his flesh is on fire.

He tries to roll over and wipe her blood off of him and onto the floor, seeking some respite from the agony. Looking down, though, he sees that he's only rubbing off great sheafs of skin along with her blood. Her spray is melting the flesh off his bones. She's turned him into a living, writhing mass of skin, sloughing itself off in clotted waves, like a burning book, its smoldering pages curling in on itself one after another.

With his dying breaths he forces the only question he can think to ask. "How...did you...find me?"

She turns then, and faces him, kneeling down to get closer. Regarding him with a pixie-like gleam in her eye, she runs her hand along his corrupted flesh. His skin oozes through her fingers, and when she raises her hand to her mouth, it runs down her arm in dripping gobs.

With a small smile that shows large pleasure, she takes a stringy rope of blood into her mouth and answers.

"It was your smell," she says, and then she begins her feast.